DEEP WITHIN THE JUNGLE

The grasses whispered gently. The sun died. After a while the sly conversation of the veldt was joined by another voice, much deeper, and more distant.

Oom, om. Oom, mm, oom, om, mn. Oom, om. Oom, mm, om, mn.

Silence. Howard Lee sat up abruptly. "What's that?"

"Drums," Kit said quietly. "What else?"

The music began again. Stahl too was listening now, intently. "What does it mean?" he asked.

"Go away," Kit said.

"Eh? Don't give me that. What does it mean?"

"That's what it means," Kit said. "*Malamu.* Go away. That's what it means."

THE NIGHT SHAPES

JAMES BLISH

AVON
PUBLISHERS OF BARD, CAMELOT, DISCUS AND FLARE BOOKS

AVON BOOKS
A division of
The Hearst Corporation
1790 Broadway
New York, New York 10019

First Avon Printing, September, 1983

AVON TRADEMARK REG. U. S. PAT. OFF. AND IN
OTHER COUNTRIES, MARCA REGISTRADA, HECHO EN
U. S. A.

Printed in the U. S. A.

WFH   10 9 8 7 6 5 4 3 2 1

I *The Residency*

The sun

It is impossible to complete the sentence. Even the centipedes are stunned. But everyone understands.

At Mushie, the Kwango and that branch of the Ikatta which drains Lake Leopold come together on their way to the Congo. It is not far to the equator, but it is impossible to imagine that the sun can become any worse.

It was here that Kit Kennedy came out of the jungle. He was not in a *balaniere*, which is the usual boat of white men on shallow waters in this country. He came out in a Bulu dugout, poled by four silent African warriors. With him was Tombu, his *capita*, or headman, and about as much gear as the usual white man would carry for a trek of a mile or so.

Kit had forty miles to go to make Berghe Ste. Marie, but he was not much of a man for gear—or for hurry. After twelve years in the Congo, his time had become jungle time, in which hours and months sometimes get mixed.

At Mushie he bought shells for his antiquated Davidson .38 and pushed off again, this time with four fresh boys and a heavy war canoe. The canoe must have been brought down the Kassai to its junction with the Juma thirty miles east, for such craft were useless along the swampy Ikatta. Where the new boys had come from could not be conjectured; Kit had not hired them in Mushie; they just appeared.

When the canoe swept around the bend into Berghe Ste. Marie, a crowd collected in a hurry, pointing and jabbering.

*"Je adjali."**
"Wapi ye?"
"Awa."
"Je makasi,"
"Je nina?"
"Mondele Ktendi."

It was a compliment to be named, though "Ktendi" did not come very close to recognizability; generally Africans simply tagged the white men—"the short fat white man," "the white man with the whip." It had been nearly a year since Kit had been this close to the Congo, and though he had been counting on the excitement, he had been none too sure that he would get it.

But apparently they remembered him well enough. Shortly they would be lining up at the Residency, trying to find out if *bwana* Ktendi would be making a safari this year. If the drums had brought him on a fool's errand, he would be able to slip away in the confusion.

The four boys sprang out of the boat at the shore and beached the canoe. Tombu did not help, the labor would have been beneath his *mpifo*, his station in the fantastically elaborated code of dignity in which even the smallest kind of job had its place.

"You will go directly to the Residency, *Mondele?*" he said.

---

*Translation of Swahili terms and phrases used throughout the text is found in the Appendix on page 123.

Kit shook his head and got out, shouldering the Davidson; Tombu followed.

"There will be Europeans," he said. "Better that I bathe, Tombu. The jungle reek sometimes offends delicate white noses."

The *capita* shrugged. His chest tattooing showed him to be a Bantu chieftain, a *nibo* or king of some small realm that the white men had not yet shattered. He knew well enough that everything has its smell. The fact that Kit Kennedy's own nose was white under its deep bronze tan did not seem to occur to him.

For that matter, it seldom occurred to Kit Kennedy. For him his own heart pumped black blood. For twelve years he had prayed at black altars, and had been given black women for *matabische*, and thought black thoughts. The mind is like the skin: under the sun, it blackens.

The woman on the veranda of the resthouse, however, worked a minor miracle; she reminded him of his Kansas upbringing. She was perched on the rickety ironwood railing, talking to a fat man Kit did not recognize, and negligently switching the tsetse flies away from firm naked legs with a palmetto fan. Kit's first reaction was African: obviously she was a newcomer; she would learn to respect the flies after a while, and change to jodhpurs. His second reaction was Western: bare legs were unheard of for a decent white woman in any part of the globe. He realized simultaneously that everything else about her was unusual also. She had close-cropped copper hair, and high, full breasts for which the thin silk of her tropical shirt did remarkable services. Kit stopped and stared.

"I don't believe a word of it," she was saying in English. Her voice was husky and provocative, but with a certain cold petulance which Kit found unpleasant. "He sounds like one of young Haggaard's characters. Allan Quartermain, perhaps. I'll wager he's a little scrawny poacher afraid of his own—"

"Seeing is believing," someone said from the doorway. The voice was familiar; it belonged to Justin

LeClerc, the *Demeurant*. "Would that you look behind yourself, Madame Lee."

The girl said "What?" and jumped down off the railing to the ground, turning in midair like a cat. Her green, startled gaze struck Kit like a thunderstone.

He continued to assay her, paying particular and obvious attention to her flat belly. She was unable to bear it for more than a moment; obviously she had expected to be ogled, but not with such undisguised particularity. She turned her back on him and went stiffly up the two steps, keeping her buttocks very taut.

Kit smiled and shifted the smoothbore off his shoulder, passing it to Tombu. He followed the girl up the steps and leaned against the worm-eaten post.

"I got your message," he said to the *Demeurant*. "I hope it's as urgent as you made it sound."

"You took your time about it," the girl said.

Kit looked at her again. No, he had not been misled by twelve years of black wives. She was indeed very beautiful; no longer a young girl, but still perfectly free of the saggings and indentations of too much experience, and full to the fingertips of that urgency which perfects women only a split second before it spoils them.

Under this sun, it would happen very rapidly if it were to happen at all. Kit did not think it would. She was very beautiful, but she was also very, very British. She wouldn't last long here.

"Mr. Kennedy has made remarkable time," LeClerc interposed smoothly. "His lodge is in Gundu country."

"I didn't hurry," Kit said in a flat voice. "As it happens, I wasn't far off when the drums brought the word. Right now I need a wash. I don't relish business hot off a trek."

"Certainly," LeClerc said. "But if you will allow me—"

"Later, please. I can see that the lady is an amateur. I'm not a guide, LeClerc." He fell back into Swahili, though Tombu's French was excellent. The girl's electric presence goaded him to be even more rude than usual. "Tell the boys we'll be leaving day after tomorrow."

"Yes, *Mondele*."

The African nodded and turned away, six feet three of quiet dignity. Something in his posture, however, made Kit think that he was enjoying himself. Evidently the woman had not impressed him, either; but then, nobody in the Negro or Arab worlds had any use for European ideas of beauty. Up north, where the faithful Allah were promised houri with faces "as round as the moon, and hips like cushions," Kit had once heard a desert chieftain describe the wife of a Danish archeologist, a girl as amply beautiful as a Valkyrie, as "the thin *sitt.*"

"It is you that makes the mistake, Kit," LeClerc said. *"M*. Stahl"—he indicated the fat, barrel-chested stranger—"is no hunter or concessionaire. It is he with whom you have your business. He is here on behalf of Belgium."

Kit scanned Stahl carefully. He had found long ago that it is simple caution to look at the human animal first as an animal; that impression, at least, will never be disappointed.

Stahl looked back, waiting, without the least apparent embarrassment. He was certainly stout, but Kit was in some doubt as to whether it was meat or fat. He was taller than he had appeared from below the veranda, and had wiry, close-cropped hair; his face was that of an abnormally intelligent butcher.

"Belgium means nothing to me," Kit said, addressing himself directly to this man. "Until Belgium begins to treat Africans as if they were human beings, I consider all Belgians a revolting crew of *gigas*—possibly excluding LeClerc, it all depends on the day. Do I make myself clear?"

"Moderately so," Stahl said in a surprisingly high voice; and Kit had an instant vision of the man getting off a boat and being swarmed over by porters and peddlers of filthy pictures; porters and peddlers both were shouting in German. *Ah!* Kit thought—indeed, he almost nodded.

"You may change your mind," Stahl was saying. "I am told that you are indispensable for my purposes, *M*. Kennedy, but I am prepared to doubt it."

"I doubt it myself, thank God."

"To be sure," Stahl said, as if automatically. "I know also that you are an American, here on a visitor's visa which is long expired. Indeed, it might be described as extinct, isn't that so?"

"Quite so," Kit said. "But not at all pertinent. If that kind of threat is all you have to offer, you're wasting your breath."

There was a stir in the shadows inside the Residency, and the girl turned.

"Ah, Howard," she said. "Come on out, and take a look at the famous Mr. Kennedy. It may be your last, it seems."

A blond man of about thirty, tall but thin, emerged onto the porch, blinking in the sudden furious light. He was extremely pale, and there was something about him that suggested the scholar. He said nothing, simply looking at Kit solemnly but in a friendly way, like Agassiz examining the fish.

"I'm well aware," Stahl was saying, "that we couldn't flush you from your jungle warrens, sir." He snuffled in the hot wet air with a sudden sharp sucking sound, like a cow pulling its foot out of thick mud, and spat over the railing. "But you would find it awkward to be reported under arrest in the settlements."

"Or shipped home," the girl added, turning her back toward Stahl.

LeClerc smiled wryly, blinking his quinine-glazed eyes.

"That," he said, "might require an army, Paula. Still Kit, consider: you need shells then and now, and also other times. Why be forced to raid for them? *M*. Stahl's project will not last forever—and he has offered excellent wages for a good guide into your part of the country. I have told him that no other white man knows it half so well. That, in fact, hardly anybody else knows it at all."

Kit looked from Stahl to the Resident to the silent Howard, and then, finally, at the girl. He was uncertain for a moment; but he had *mpifo* of his own to maintain. What you did then, the sorcerers said, was to lay everything on the air.

"I leave day after tomorrow," he said.

The air, which was quite thick enough to float a flatiron, took the burden without noticing.

The next morning, like the previous morning, and all previous mornings since the world was born, was bloody and stifling; world without end. By the time Stahl and the Resident had appeared, chattering with businesslike affability about administrative matters and procedures about as applicable to the back side of the Moon as to the Congo, Kit was too busy battling off would-be *askaris* to bother asking Stahl where he was going and what he wanted there. Tombu, having gotten a good look at the girl—nothing to him, African and a king, but he knew his boss very well—had not bothered to countermand the orders he had given out yesterday. Consequently, when Kit went out to announce that there would be a safari after all, he found the compound already filled with eager, gesticulating Bulus from half a dozen nearby villages.

"You're to blame for this, Tombu," he told the grinning warrior. "For *matabische,* you may pick them over yourself. Make sure you get nothing but the best. I don't want ivory-hunters' boys."

"Mpo-kuseya," Tombu said ritually. "I cannot fail." Since he also could not quite stop grinning, he turned away.

"Tika," Kit said. "I haven't finished. Tell them we will be going toward Balalondzy. That will thin them out in a hurry."

Tombu's grin faded a little.

"This is not true, *Mondele?"*

"And suppose it is?"

"Then we go," Tombu said evenly. "It will be a quiet safari—you, and I, and the whites— and *mokele-mbemba."*

Kit smiled. Tombu had seen his point well enough.

"Let *mokele-mbemba* sleep on the bottom of the Ssombo with the white hippo," he said. He slapped the big Bantu's shoulder. "It is a fiction, Tombu. Go spread it."

Tombu strode away. Kit gazed after him thoughtfully. Another man might have pulled at an ear lobe

or rubbed his chin, but Kit had no nervous mannerisms;
they had been sweated out of him, or left behind. Now
when there was something on his mind, he stood still
and thought about it; he had learned from the cats that
tail-switching is a hunting lure, not an aid to thought.

Mokele-mbemba. It was an old Congo legend, but it
cropped up as far away as the Cameroons and the Blue
Nile. Even there, one heard reports of a great, gray-
brown beast, with green and yellow mottlings. It had
the head of a lizard, the neck of a giraffe, the body of
a hippo, the tail of a snake . . . a proper chimera, lacking
only breasts and wings; but the tallies were remarkably
consistent. If one imagined it into being, the image was
worthy to be matched against the prehistoric reptiles
in Lyly's newly published *Elements of Geology*. An old
monster, an instance of special creation perhaps, or perhaps only a myth, as fully half the animals in Lyly had
to be.

But the reports seldom varied. Europeans scoffed at
them; Kit did not. Nor, for that matter, did any experienced hunter or guide. The swamps of Africa con-
cealed stranger things; so did the seas; off Madagascar
one could catch fishes, now and then, which would have
been incredible even to Lyly, had he ever seen one. In
the Comores, the natives called them *Kombessa,* and
ate them, though not with relish. The cane-brakes and
reeds could hide anything, no matter what its size,
within fifteen feet, were it hippogriff, phoenix, chimera,
sphinx, roc, dragon, sea serpent, or the web-footed Apoc-
alypse itself. In such cases, it was better to put one's
credit in the legends; common sense was no man's guide
here. One lived longer that way.

As Kit stood quietly looking away from the compound, the door to the rest-house banged to, and Stahl
came back out into the sunlight, blinking rapidly. After
a surprisingly short moment he spotted Kit and came
stumping toward him, like a wine keg on stilts. It was
still early in the morning, no more than reasonably
muggy, but Stahl's shirt was already patched with sweat.
Just to look at the man made Kit itch.

Of this Stahl was quite oblivious.

"When shall you be ready, Mr. Kennedy?" he said

at once. "I am quite informed that my detachment of
marines arrived by last night's packet. The sooner we
are able to start—"

"Marines?" Kit said. "What do you need marines for?
Nobody mentioned marines to me. What do you plan,
anyhow—a punitive expedition?"

"Perhaps," Stahl said. "That remains to be seen. The
Colonial Office has received some odd reports from up
north—tales of illegal mining, and other things."

Kit's lips thinned.

"Up-country is full of tales," he said. "It's very difficult to get bearers to go in there. Furthermore, the
tribes there have no reason to love whites. If you go in
there with a company of marines, you'll very like not
come out again. The tribes want guns."

"That's quite enough," Stahl said sharply. "I'm in
charge of this expedition, Mr. Kennedy. I assure you I
have reasons for what I do—"

He broke off. A tall, slender young man in marine
uniform was striding toward them from the docks.

"There's Captain van Bleyswijck," he said. "See me
later, please."

Kit shrugged and moved off, out of what a European
would have considered earshot. Behind him, however,
he heard nothing informative. The marine and Stahl
were muttering to each other in Walloon, a language
of which he had almost no experience.

His nostrils flared; this whole business almost literally smelled. Yet he could not put his finger on what
was wrong.

Up-country? Then his mock threat of Balalondzy had
in fact come close to the mark. And whether *mokele-
mbemba* was real or not, there was almost certainly
some kind of epidemic savaging that swamp-ridden area.
Kit had seen some of the leperous refugees, big-bellied
and thin-blooded as though with the *kwashiorkor*, tortured with oozing, unhealing lesions not at all like those
of tropical ulcer, shunned by the Gundu tribes, driven
from barred *bomas* to die in the jungle, or sometimes
to be brought down by emboldened hyenas even before
they were properly dead.

What could Stahl want up there? What could be up

there that needed a marine squad to take it, and to take it out? Certainly not ivory—it couldn't be transported.

Abruptly he turned and went into the Residency. LeClerc, as usual, was sitting at his desk over a tumbler of whiskey, a potion which looked like water, and tasted to Kit as though it had been drained out of a latrine. He was stirring some papers in his hands, but not looking at them; instead, he was watching the progress of a lizard down the wall next to him. The reptile was stalking a beetle almost half its size.

His gaze snapped to Kit quickly enough, however, and he smiled.

"Ah," he said, and tossed down the rest of the Dutch gin expertly. "I was hoping you'd come back."

"I can't see why," Kit said. "The way you people have been breaking your necks giving me information, I'd assumed you'd prefer I stayed out of sight and kept my mouth shut."

The Resident sighed and spread his hands. "Kit, I agree with you, this odd project began badly. Newcomers are slow to understand this country, not so? But I assure you, it is all perfectly legitimate. I have had letters, I can show them to you—some of them."

"But what's it all about, LeClerc? Wouldn't it be more sensible to tell me?"

"There are several purposes, naturally," the Resident said, pawing among his papers. Perhaps he was looking for the letters he had mentioned, but if so, he did not seem to be having much luck. "One doesn't send an expedition upriver for only one reason, it is hardly economical. This one is mainly medical, I gather."

"Medical? Stahl's a medico? Well, that makes a little sense."

"No, not Stahl, Dr. Lee. Young as he is, he is an authority on tropical diseases. I have checked his *bona fides.*"

Kit thought about it. They needed a doctor up-country, of that he was already more than aware. If the silent young Englishman was a real expert, so much the better.

"And Stahl?"

"That," the Resident said with seemingly genuine

regret, "I cannot divulge, Kit. His mission too is legitimate, I give you my most fervent assurances, but I have been asked officially not to say more. I will tell you this: Doctor Lee has not been told this matter, either. There are good reasons. How can I say more?"

Abruptly, Kit stopped worrying about it. He had no choice about going, in any event, and the pay was good enough. As for the girl....

There was trouble in even thinking about that, but he was determined to discover what the hell she was doing in this peculiar expedition.

It was a silent and a tense trek, that first afternoon. The sun disappeared as soon as they were out of sight of Berghe Ste. Marie, but you knew it was there above the trees and the coiled vines; the air, motionless, was like live steam. Within the hour the boys had discarded their loincloths, but beyond that nothing was normal; there was none of the usual chanting, nor even any small talk among the whites.

The boys Tombu had hired had all seemed eager enough to travel with Ktendi—at first. It was not hard to guess where their enthusiasm had gone.

The presence of the marines made it worse, as Kit had known it would. The bearers were not surly yet, but they were suspicious. Kit caught several questioning glances thrown his way and was thoroughly aware that Tombu was sensitive to the undercurrent of dissatisfaction also.

Stahl had wanted to stomp along at the head of the party. Kit had had some difficulty in persuading him that the scouts should go first. Every step brought them closer to hippo and swamp-boar territory, and an inexperienced man could run squarely into death without knowing it was there.

Stahl's experience was dubious, to say the least. As for Dr. Lee, he seemed simply inefficient; if he had ever had any field experience with tropical diseases, it must have been acquired in Egypt or Asia Minor, not in a jungle. He was clearly trying not to be any trouble, but the boys were constantly bailing him out of the most obvious minor pitfalls. In between mishaps, he asked Kit medical questions which Kit was unable to answer,

not, usually for want of the answers, but because the
questions were couched in a clinical jargon so ferocious
that Kit couldn't be sure what the owl-eyed man was
getting at. His anxiety about his gear would have been
pathetic had Kit not himself been urgently aware of
how valuable it was. Indeed, it was thus far the only
reason for the whole hegira that Kit had been allowed
to know.

The girl swung along easily. She wore featherweight
breeches and a twill shirt, a good compromise between
the heat and the insects. Kit was surprised to see how
well she took to trekking. Even the boys' nakedness
had not taken her aback, apparently. She was not be-
having at all like a protected British maiden, though
there were signs that she had never been on a pro-
tracted safari before, either.

For that matter, Stahl did not act much like a Belgian field official, let alone anyone who knew more
about the Congo than could be gotten out of some book
(very probably that same piece of trash full of elephants'
graveyards and other fictions that all tourists seemed
to have memorized). And young van Bleyswijck, the
marine captain, was a curiously stiff type, almost pro-
fessorial for a soldier. He was completely unwilling to
speak to anyone but Stahl, Paula, and his sergeant;
Tombu and the boys visibly made him nervous. Yet he
moved with the automatic caution of an experienced
guide or hunter, and had an almost reflex knowledge
of which jungle sounds to ignore.

Enigmas, all of them; of the group, Captain van
Bleyswijck puzzled Kit most. After a while, obscurely
bored with watching and listening to him murmuring
in Paula's ear, Kit slowed down his pace slightly to let
them catch up to him.

Van Bleyswijck froze up at once and moved off. Kit
held his ground, however. Talking with a white woman,
especially a beautiful one, was an almost unknown experience on safari; and besides, Kit could not wait much
longer to find out why this particular safari was so off-
odor.

If he had other reasons, he kept them from himself.
He had had practice.

"You're Herr Stahl's secretary, I gather," he said.

She looked at him obliquely, fending off a palmetto frond which came switching stiffly back from van Bleyswijck's warding hand into her face.

"Herr Stahl?" she said. "Why the German title?"

Kit felt a vague annoyance at being put on the defensive with such prompt deftness.

"Why not?" he said. "It's an intuition. He doesn't seem like the Belgian type to me. Have you known him long?"

"About a year," she said. "He's Belgian. Officially, anyhow. The Colonial Office acknowledges him; that's good enough."

"Oh? Then you weren't sure yourself at first?"

She smiled.

"I had no interest in the matter one way or the other," she said. "I'm an attaché of the British Admiralty, Mr. Kennedy, loaned out to Sir Edward Grey's office—over the very stiffnecked protests of my family. They thought it was dreadfully unfeminine of me to obtain work in the Admiralty in the first place; now they believe that Her Majesty's Government is as mad as I am. But under the circumstances, of course, there was nothing they could do."

It took Kit a moment to realize that this was no answer at all, but only a smooth evasion; she had answered his first question instead of his second. It was an interesting performance; his respect for her rose, unwillingly.

"I'd rather you lied to me directly," Kit said. "What circumstances?"

The girl flushed slightly.

"I'm not Stahl's secretary," she said stiffly. "I'm Howard Lee's wife. Which is neither here nor there, Mr. Kennedy. I am also a graduate pathologist—one of the six or eight in the world. I studied under Virchow. That's why I'm here—and it's entirely sufficient."

"Perhaps it is," Kennedy said gravely. "Thank you."

She sniffed and stopped walking, waiting for van Bleyswijck to catch up with her. Kit let her fall back; he had a lot to think over. He shot a quick look at Dr. Lee.

The man should not have caught it, but somehow he did, and smiled back, hesitantly. The response was shy but direct, without any trace of jealousy that Kit could detect. In fact, there had been *no* sign thus far that Lee and Paula were married—they barely spoke to one another, and certainly showed no concern over each other's welfare. Was she lying? She was good at that, as Kit had just discovered; but why tell a lie so easy to check? There was no artistry in that.

However, it was probably true that she was a pathologist; it fitted, and helped the expedition to make a little more sense. For the rest, there was nothing more to be learned from her at the moment, that was clear enough. He was content to wait until later, to hear what more she would say under stress.

It was bound to be interesting. Nothing about Paula Lee was ordinary; the truth, when it came out, ought to be worth hearing.

The safari debouched into a small clearing, tufted underfoot with mosses, but not insecure to the feet. Blades of sunlight as sharp as spears of stained glass pierced to the turf, and clouds of gnats danced in them, gnats so tiny as to make distinct segments of rainbows with their wings in the farthest beams.

Kit shaded his eyes and scanned the patches of sky visible through the convolvuli, his back to the sun. A faint mistiness in the light told him that Lake Wassabi was not far off, at least by his own standards of march. Ordinarily, one of the Wassabi tribes would have met him here to swap gifts and information. This time, it was as though they were being shunned. The jungle was very quiet.

It would continue to be quiet, Kit knew. There were still no drums. The progress of the safari was being told in some other way—a way not open to eavesdropping by Ktendi and Tombu. It was, in its way, a grim compliment: there was not another white man in Africa who would be suspected of the ability to hear words in the drum music—which, in point of fact, Kit could do only imperfectly in most dialects.

The girl stopped at his side and looked up as well, but it only made her squint.

"Where are we?"

"We're about a day along. I make it about another three days of clear going. After that we'll have to slow down."

"That doesn't tell me anything."

"Very well," Kit said. "What's this about Sir Edward Grey? The last time I saw a newspaper he'd just been appointed. The Congo Reform Commission—little enough will come of *that*, with Belgium represented! What did they send you here for? To make a gesture?"

The girl said nothing. Kit watched her intently. Her reserve was cold enough by European standards, but Kit was used to assessing the expressions of the most impassive faces in the world. The minute flickers of facial muscles beneath her smooth skin were enough for him; she might as well have had her thoughts tattooed on her forehead.

It is none of his business. Still, he has a right to ask. He might even have guessed more than I have.

"You don't know what you're here for, yourself," he said disgustedly. "At least you're none too sure."

She stared at him, startled.

"What are you talking about?" she said. "Of course I'm sure. I have full instructions."

"To do what? To cooperate with, to lend the fullest assistance to, to watch for the best interests of, to make a detailed report to—? That's not a set of instructions, it's a recipe."

A hit. The girl's lower lip tensed slightly.

"I am not anybody's equerry, Mr. Kennedy," she said. "I have instructions."

"To watch Stahl, and find out what he's up to."

Her lips thinned again, and her nostrils flared slightly. No, Kit thought, that's not it—but it's uncomfortably close.

"Nonsense," she said briskly. "As far as I'm concerned, Stahl is all right. A bit choleric, that's all. I'm here to help Howard, and to check on the enforcement of the Reform Edicts. So is he, I presume. There have been reports of illegal mining up north and slavery; that's why van Bleyswijck is here."

"It all sounds stupid to me," Kit said.

"Oh, indeed?"

"Indeed. Remember, I live here. Of course there's slavery up north; slavery and slaughter are the rule here. But it's tribal, nobody's exporting it—it would be impossible to get white slavers up that far. And if van Bleyswijck thinks he can extirpate slavery between the tribes with a squad of marines, he knows less about the Congo than I think he does."

"I see. You know everything. The illegal mining is also nonsense, of course."

Kit shrugged.

"Nobody in his right mind tries to do any mining in swampland," he said. "The natives up there dig peat, but that's all. There's gold in the interior, certainly, and plenty of it—a big deposit lies right at my back door. But that's in the Basin. Around Balalondzy there's nothing but stink."

"You still have something to learn," Paula said enigmatically. "Why are you living here, anyhow, if there's so much gold for the taking where you are?"

"It's very simple. I like it here. There's nothing outside Africa that I could buy with gold." For an instant, he saw again the yellow-framed face above the long waves of Kansas wheat, a vision ethereal and terrifying. In his mind, a door closed over it with a soundless, shocking concussion. "I use a little ore to swap for shells now and then. But what I really want, I have to work for, because it can't be bought."

"And what's that?" she said, regarding him with puzzled interest.

For once Kit was off guard; the vision was gone, but the shock of it left behind filled him too full of alarm to leave room for caution; he spoke without thinking.

"To be left alone, mostly," he said.

Even then, although he knew that he had spoken, he did not properly hear what he had said until minutes later.

II *The Marches*

On the fourth day, as Kit had predicted, the country began to change.

The terrific humidity of the coastal shelf did not fall off, but gradually it took on a heavy, fetid smell, like being downwind of an elephant herd. The broad aisles of baobab and shea trees tangled and vanished, leaving the safari hacking its way among close-set, scaly doum-palms. The ground was spongy underfoot, and the moss grew in shaky tussocks, between which pursed the carnivorous little kisses of the flytraps.

The flies themselves were maddening. There were far more of them than was usual in swampy country. Evidently the sickening odor was indeed evidence of considerable carrion somewhere.

After the fifth hour of this kind of travel, van Bleyswijck's boots were full of muddy seepage and his face and arms were blotched an angry red. Above all, he seemed to be losing his temper. Finally he broke, and spoke directly to Kit, for the first time.

"Wouldn't we do better if we veered east?" he panted, slashing viciously at a tough liana.

"I don't know," Kit said. He spoke briefly to Tombu.

"*Ay-obwa*," Tombu said, shrugging. "*Bendele bafa banto.*"

"Tombu says nothing is wrong," Kit said, forbearing to translate Tombu's additional opinion of Bleyswijck's difficulties—*White men are not people.* "I think it's like this all the way."

"Well, it's damnable. I wish we could get on higher ground."

Kit was half right. It got hotter, but on the fifth day the ground began to tip upward and drain a little. Tombu skinned his way to the top of a palm, and thereafter reported a day's climb ahead—whether to a new jungle, or to a series of foothills of some unknown mountain range, he could not tell. The fringe of swamp they had crossed evidently was a sink or gutter, but they might well hit it again on the other side.

Kit called a halt, to Stahl's intense annoyance.

"What's the delay?" he fumed, fat hands on his hips. "You don't seem to realize, Mr. Kennedy, that this expedition is urgent."

"And you," Kit said evenly, "don't seem to realize that we have a totally new situation to meet here. This area's never been mapped, and there may be mountains ahead. We aren't equipped to scale a range of any size."

"Why not?"

"Evidently you've never seen mountains in Africa. They aren't worn down to nubbins, like the Alps, you know. Most of them are new—great unweathered block-piles as raw as the mountains of the moon. I myself have seen one thirty thousand feet high."

"There is no such mountain," Stahl snorted. "Everest isn't as high as that."

"Everest is too old. I know what I saw. And I know how to triangulate, Stahl."

"There'll be trails through any mountain range," Stahl said. "There are natives in this region—or so you said."

"Even if there are trails," Kit said patiently, "we don't have supplies enough to cross a big range. We'll save time and trouble by sending back now for rope and food and about fifteen more boys."

"Nonsense!" Stahl shouted. "I won't have it, do you hear? There probably aren't any mountains anyhow. I insist that we go on!"

Tombu stepped silently closer, switching the *sjambok* questioningly against his thigh, but Kit shook his head. He had to avoid making an incident at all costs; it would be impossible to explain to the African the complex and, to the *nibo*, inconsequential paper club of the passport which Stahl held over him, with the assistance of the *Demeurant*. If Stahl wanted to climb under-manned and under-equipped in hostile country, he'd have to be allowed to do it. Tombu looked puzzled and a little disappointed.

But then, perhaps Stahl would fall on something and get killed. That, at least, would amuse Tombu; he liked jokes.

"That seems sensible," Paula said. "After all, we may be just borrowing trouble. And it shouldn't take more than an hour to get up where we can see for ourselves, one way or the other."

"A day, the native says," van Bleyswijck said morosely. "Two days would be more like it, if it keeps up like this."

As it turned out, the marine was close. It was almost dusk of the next day when the safari struck reasonably level ground. Up here the doum-palms thinned in their turn, frond by frond, trunk by scaly trunk. The turf was solid and dry, almost dusty, and the heat came along the air in long slow waves, so much less moist as to counterfeit a breeze. Their flesh slowly turned sticky; Paula kept falling back to pull her clothes free of her body, and Stahl was openly scratching, which he would regret very shortly. At least there were fewer flies, however.

Despite the deepening sky, a pearly light began to show between the tree trunks. Stahl forgot to scratch and stared.

"Look!" he crowed. "See! Open territory! Your impassible barrier was a myth, Mr. Kennedy."

"Was it?" Kit said.

He pushed ahead. In the dimming light he could see the silhouettes of his two scouts, standing silent and serious at what seemed to be the edge of the forest. They stepped aside to let the party file into the open.

Ahead of them stretched fantastic and desolate country—a flat, unrelieved plateau dotted here and there with the contorted shapes of dragon trees, grown waist-high in elephant grass. The grass moved with the heat ... *the long waves crossed the sea of wheat, the face blazed and faded. . . .*

Kit shook his head violently and stared ahead. The face had vanished. Almost beyond his range of vision, where the face had been, was a looming violet wall which shut off the hazy horizon: a single, flat-topped mountain, its height impossible to estimate at this shadowless hour, flanked by tumbles of cliffs smaller but cruelly sheer.

"Which way is Balalondzy?" Howard Lee whispered.

Kit gestured northwest, his face troubled.

"Over there—but the way's cut off. I wonder what made van Bleyswijck suggest our working east? It looks like the only way to get around that thing. What about this country, Tombu?"

"Bad," Tombu said. "Lions, perhaps. Thorn trees. Snakes."

Kit nodded.

"It looks like veldt, all right. Odd country for the Congo; I'll never learn all there is to know here. Better unship the guns."

Tombu swung to the porters. *"Bondoki!"* he shouted.

Cases thudded to the ground, and the askaris broke them open. The marines began cleaning their own rifles with apprehensive efficiency.

Stahl was giving a reasonable imitation of a toad about to burst. Kit peered judiciously into his smoothbore, which was as usual very clean, and ignored him.

"Verdamn!" Stahl roared. "Who gifs oud orders here? Bode of us cannot gommand dis eggspedition!"

He dashed at Tombu and dealt the astonished man a heavy blow on the ear. Tombu got his balance back by moving one foot, and quietly grasped the whip in his hand where its thongs left the handle. There was a lump of ironstone under the withes of the grip.

"Put dose guns avay!" Stahl was shouting, staring at Tombu with blind eyes. "If we are addacked—"

Kit was upon him in two strides. He grabbed the man's shoulder, spun him around, and threw him heavily against a tree trunk.

"You god-damned pig," he growled in English. He clenched his teeth and got a little of his control back. "Stahl, you're a fool. This grassland is nine times worse than any possible jungle you've seen up to now. Do you *want* to cross it alone?"

"I vill not haf dese savages armed," Stahl raged, glaring at Kit. "If dey should turn on us—"

"They won't," Kit said. "They all know me. They won't use the rifles against us, no matter what happens. I once lost ten good boys because I was afraid to trust them with guns. I don't mean to see it happen again— not for any price. Let alone for a piece of paper, Stahl. Understand?"

Stahl looked into Kit's face, sputtering; evidently what he saw convinced him, at least for the moment. The sputtering subsided. When he spoke again, his accent was utterly obliterated; his French had once more its slight Flemish tang. But about the pitch of his voice he could do nothing, and he acknowledged it with his sixth word.

"You think more of these *Neger* than you do of us," he grumbled.

This was so obvious that Kit did not bother to agree, let alone to deny it. He set about supervising the making of camp.

The grasses whispered gently. The sun died. After a while the sly conversation of the veldt was joined by another voice, much deeper, and more distant.

Oom, om. Oom, mm, oom, om, mn. Oom, om. Oom, mm, om, mn.

Silence.

Oom, om. Oom, mm, oom, om, mn.

At first, no one but Kit and the boys heard it. Here and there, they rose on their elbows. Tombu scooped up a double handful of dust and held it cupped between his tailor-folded knees, looking at the fire as he listened.

Oom, om. Oom, mm, oom, om, mn.

Silence.

Howard Lee sat up abruptly.

"What's that?"

"Drums," Kit said quietly. "What else?"

"But where?"

"Across there somewhere. Maybe in the foothills. Shut up a minute."

The music began again, the speech-music that followed faithfully the natural melody of a Swahili sentence. Since the drums could not form words, each word in a drum-sentence had to speak the melody of a word-sentence, to fix its context; you cannot say "woman" alone in drum-language, you must say "The woman will never go to the *linginda*", and then you know, for women are not allowed to fish with that net.

Stahl too was listening now, intently, like a fat mouse waiting for a cat's footfall.

"What do they say?" he asked huskily.

"If you don't shut up, I won't be able to make it out," Kit said.

Silence.

Oom, om. Oom, mm, oom, om, mn.

"Ah," Kit said to himself. "*Malamu*, Tombu. Is that the word?"

"*Ayah, bondele.*"

"What's that?" Stahl said. "What does that mean?"

"'Go away,'" Kit said.

"Eh? Don't give me that. What does it mean?"

"That's what it means," Kit said. "*Malamu*. Go away. That's what it means."

For a long time after the party had bedded down—the Africans with that crude fatalism which, coming with darkness, made them such easy prey for slavers; the whites with their absurd nerves which anticipated for tomorrow what could not be less than a week away—Kit sat at the base of the tree he had picked out for himself, the Davidson in his lap, and looked out over the starlit grassland. Over the dark plateau was a whole wheel and whirlpool of stars: it was that galaxy which, spilling out from Andromeda over nearly half the sky, is never seen by the naked eye unless that eye looks up from a whole continent of lightlessness. Even now, Kit could see only its hazy spiral heart, for to his right a small watch-fire burned, not entirely shielded from his peripheral vision by the tents huddled around it.

Kit hated watch-fires. He also hated tents. To his taste, nothing matched a tall, thin-boled tree for sleeping quarters—a tree whose nearest branches were beyond the leap of a big cat, and whose trunk was pliant enough to bend rather than snap to the charge of a heavier animal. As for snakes—Kit had shared perches with snakes more than once, and found them uniformly timid; the trick was not to move too suddenly, that was all.

Human beings, particularly white ones, were not so dependable. Kit sat still, listening to the distant *girot* throbbing out his tireless word of menace on the skins. There must be a fire burning there, too, or the night dew would have long ago relaxed the drums to uselessness; the silence between the sentence-words were growing longer, as the *girot* paused to heat the heads.

That made sense; but what the whites were up to was as cloudy as ever. Above all, what could Stahl be after? Nothing he had done thus far fitted with anything else, unless you assumed that he was trying to commit suicide.

First, he had taken a ridiculously small force of marines into country he knew to be both hostile and nearly impassible.

He had refused to send for reinforcements or extra supplies when the going became threatening.

He had antagonized his head boy—deliberately, Kit was convinced.

He had tried to prohibit the distribution of arms, at the most dangerous point in the trip.

And though he had forced Kit to accompany him upon threat of having the American placed under arrest, he had failed to threaten that arrest again when Kit had crossed him—and roughed him up in the process.

And what about van Bleyswijck? Theoretically, he was along to protect Stahl; yet he had not made any move when Kit had opposed Stahl directly, either to guard Stahl's person or to enforce Stahl's orders.

Furthermore, Kit remembered suddenly, van Bleyswijck had twice been right about terrain which was supposed to be unknown to everyone in the party.

Tombu was right: *bendele bafa banto.* Or if they were people, they were mad.

In the distance, a new, steady beat was added to the low, intermittent tune of the message drums. It had no note and no rhythmic pattern; only a steady thud, quite without meaning. The instrument that created it must have been huge, to carry so toneless a noise over such a distance.

It could only be a work drum. Accustomed though he was to the callousness with which forced labor was put to use in the Free State, Kit was surprised and disquieted to hear the dull, brain-pulping sound of its brutal heart thudding away at night this far in the interior. Even the *Fondation de la couronne,* whose domain the territory was, had had little success in gaining any real jurisdiction over the Kasai country—and in any event the major concessionnaire here, the American Congo Company, was a rubber corporation which would hardly have any use for a work drum, let alone be tapping trees at night. The sound and the hour were both more characterstic of the *Société internationale forestière et minière du Congo;* but that made just as little sense, for what could that company be doing that Stahl would have to investigate on the spot? After all, the whole *Domaine de la couronne* was Leopold II's personal property, and the Free State was either a shareholder or a profit-sharer in all the concession companies.

For that matter, the whole understaffed "investigation" was a mystery. The last commission of investigation, under Janssens, had been an honest enough affair in itself, and an extensive one, which from October of 1904 to February of last year had managed to get itself as far up the river as Stanleyville—a not inconsiderable distance for green hands to travel in a little under five months. Their report, which had been

published only last November, had not gotten into Kit's
hands until six months later, and it had filled him with
a futile bitterness.

Oh, it had been honest enough, especially in its con-
demnation of the "sentry" system, the inhuman work
requirements of the concession companies, the suppres-
sion of free trade, and the wholesale flouting of the land
laws; but while on the one hand it insisted on the enforcement of the law limiting native labor to forty hours
a month per man—difficult to the point of impossibility
even if undertaken in entire good faith—on the other
it made its recommendation a joke by endorsing both
the concessions system and the principle of the *corvee*.
And the whole document was intolerably, boringly *gen-
eral* in its tone and approach, as somebody in Leopold's
government had taken pains to insure by printing it
shorn of the evidence which the commissioners had collected.

Naturally nothing had been done, though there was
a lot of talk, particularly in the Belgian parliament,
which had managed to kick the subject around the
chamber for five straight days before deciding on a res-
olution to "examine" a law proposed for the Congo back
in 1901. The king had subsequently issued a few decrees
which nobody would regard as serving any purpose but
that of delaying any further action, and there the matter stood still, so far as Kit's old news could inform him.
If the intervention of Sir Edward Grey were to make
any difference, the Congo would not see it for years to
come, and even that Kit was thoroughly disinclined to
believe. The Belgians would never let go.

Or what if they did? There would be hell to pay; but
it would make small difference to Kit Kennedy, a stateless person in a state of anarchy. An African Congo
would be impossible for the whites and for the Africans
themselves a worse hell than it was now, but even that
Kit could survive; he had proved it in the interior, which
effectively existed just as it always had. In any event
he had no choice. For him, Kansas no longer existed,
whereas Africa, black, white or green, was like a tattoo
on the still face of eternity.

Unbidden, he saw once more the long waves of the

wind moving over a sea of wheat, and the laughing face
above it. He had been a schoolteacher then—incredible!
Yet there he was, a stiff youngster in a high celluloid
collar, straight out of Cambridge and the only teacher
in hundreds of square miles of prairie, madly trying to
impress Greek and Latin upon farm children who could
hardly speak English. At home, they spoke Bohemian;
he had learned it, but had never since found any use
for it.

Mavra had learned from the stiff young man, and so
much for learning. She had been little interested in
Greek, but she had been lonely, like the stiff young
man, and together they had studied all the conjugations
of *amo*. She was fifteen when her pregnancy began to
show.

Kit had no friends, but Mavra's parents were unexpectedly kind. They paid out good money, in a bad
crop year, to have him tarred, feathered and railed, and
thus he got away; without their good offices, he would
have been gelded and hung. But he had not appreciated
it at the time, and out of his bitterness, one thing had
led to another, until he had come to rest here, without
a passport or even a decent pseudonym—for the United
States cared enough about preventing his re-entry to
break his assumed identities to matter where he was,
and now that he was a legend he no longer bothered to
try. He had changed; the past was no longer even pro-
logue, but only a pain-charged myth.

A slight stir nearby snapped Kit's attention closer
to home. There it was again: a movement in the bush.

Someone was trying to stalk him—and being incredibly clumsy about it.

He slid the Davidson off his lap in a smooth, silent
motion, and tensed. The minute cracklings of dry brush
came closer, and then stopped.

Kit waited. He had plenty of time. After a rather
short while, a soft shuffling of leaves whispered just
behind his back.

He shot up one arm. His fingers locked on a wiry
wrist. The hand to which it belonged had been pressing
against the tree-bole.

Kit yanked, forcing his right leg hard against the

turf at the same time, his left arm lashing behind him
to pull the stalker's foot away. Something firm and
heavy came lurching down across his shoulders. He
flung himself bodily backward.

The other hit hard under his back with a harsh
squeak, like a piglet rolled upon by a sow. Kit found a
fresh pivot point with his foot and swiveled his hips
and shoulders, hearing the smoothbore thump softly
into the dust with oddly detached regret; now he would
have to clean it again. Then the brief struggle was
frozen into panting immobility, with Kit's knees in the
small of the stalker's back, his arms drawing the other's
hands high and across.

Except for the single thud and explosion of breath,
the struggle had been completely silent. Kit held the
other's chin crammed into the dust until he was sure
there had been no alarm in the camp. Tombu had doubtless heard the whole thing and accurately deduced what
was up from the few sound cues alone, but the African
king allowed Kit to fight his own battles; that was *mpifo*.
The whites were obviously still unconscious of the whole
business.

Carefully, Kit shifted his knees until they rested on
the other's shoulders. The figure was a small one; Kit
wondered briefly if the tribe across the veldt was pigmy.
He freed one hand to yank the stalker's head sideways
before it choked.

"Never stalk a man standing," he said softly in
French. "Only fools and Europeans hunt upright."

The figure underneath him coughed indignantly.

"Get off me, you drayhorse," it said in English.
"You've already broken most of my favorite bones."

The voice was Paula's. Kit's muscles went suddenly
watery. He let go and almost jumped away.

"Excuse me," he said stiffly. "I'm sorry. I thought—"

Paula rolled over and sat up, one breast gleaming
from her torn shirt in the dying light of the watch-fire's
embers.

"You thought!" she said hoarsely, and sneezed, muf-
fling it at the last moment. "You—you're all reflexes.
If you're thinking, it must be painful."

She suppressed another sneeze, and glared at him

through the darkness. He doubted that she could see him very well. He tried to repress a chuckle, without much success.

"If you have to sneeze, then sneeze," he said in a low voice. "If you keep pinching it back you'll go on sneezing until Doomsday. Go ahead, you won't wake anybody—it's a normal animal sound."

In the next instant he almost regretted the advice. The girl said "Damn you" in a strangled voice and then unloosed a paroxysm worthy of a baby hippo. For a few moments afterward she could do nothing but snuffle and wipe her eyes.

"It's your own fault, Mrs. Lee," Kit said. "Why didn't you walk around in front of me, instead of sneaking up on me as if I were a sleeping elephant?"

"I didn't want to be seen." She sniffed again, and then belatedly put her clothes back in order, to Kit's regret, crossing her legs tailor-fashion. "As you already know very well."

"What makes you think so?"

"You said I wouldn't wake anybody if I sneezed, didn't you?"

This was undeniable; it had to be allowed that she was acute. Kit nodded once.

"I'd like to talk to you," she added. "If you think you can keep from throwing me around."

"Go ahead."

There was a brief silence. Then she said:

"Don't you know what this trip is for? Really?"

"Nobody has broken his neck running information my way," Kit said drily. "But I have a guess or two. Somebody up here is taking money out of Uncle Leopold's pocket. Uncle Leopold doesn't like poachers—hence the marines. You and your husband may well be on a bona fide medical expedition but you are probably also functioning as a cover for Stahl. In any case, Stahl is trying to jam his hand into the till."

"Do you know what's being mined?"

"No," Kit said. "I didn't know anything was being mined. Whatever it is, it must be something extremely valuable, evidently, and not too hard to smuggle. Not gold, or ivory either. What is it?"

"Don't let Stahl find out that you know—or that I told you."

"I won't promise," Kit said. "What is it?"

The girl stirred uneasily. Kit waited patiently. At last she said:

"Well, it's—"

He heard no more than that. There was a hoarse, strangled cry from near the fire. One of the boys was struggling to his feet, staggering away from the coals with legs almost out of control, hands plucking at his chest. In the next instant the darkness howled with a hundred demon voices and the pounding of a dozen drums.

Bushed!

Kit sprang up with a curse. This was what came of relaxing vigilance for a second.

"Tombu!" he shouted. "Put out that fire!"

Tombu was already in sight, running doubled-over across the clearing. He kicked at the coals, and a cloud of dust dropped from his hands on them. A flight of heavy war arrows whistled over his jackknifed body like bloodthirsty cranes. The drums seemed to be right at Kit's ears. Over the howling, a woman's voice was screaming in the darkness:

"*Ayang, ayang!*"

A *woman's* voice! Now what—

From the marine encampment rifles began to crackle. Kit gritted his teeth and yanked Paula to her feet. About all that the Belgians could do in this darkness was to hit other members of the party. Certainly the attacking tribe would not be frightened off by the sound of gunfire—the guns were almost surely just what they were after, the sound of the firing would be as maddening as the chink of gold to them—

Something landed on Kit's shoulder with all the impact of a quarter-ton leopard, and clung. Kit lurched back up to one knee and jackknifed, snatching his knife from his boot. Hands slammed around his throat. He slashed sideways and back with all his strength—

There was a bubbling scream and the hands were snatched away. Kit jerked the knife free. A gush of hot, sticky fluid spurted over his knuckles. He kicked out;

the sound of a bursting rib told him where to aim next. The man's head sounded to the toe of his boot like a thick gourd. He swung around.

"Paula? Paula!"

"Ayang, ayang!"

An arrow thunked into the tree over Kit's head. The gunfire stopped abruptly. Around the scattered fire, shadows writhed and danced like mantelpiece sculpture sprung to obscene life. In the brush, someone was kicking out, fiercely. Then Paula's voice cried out:

"Kit! Kit! I'm—"

The sound was cut off. Kit knocked the arrow free of the scaly tree-bole and shinnied up it with the ungraceful dispatch of a grandfather chimpanzee. At the first branch, he worked his way out until he seemed to be over the struggle. He could hear heavy breathing and an occasional guttural word, but except for the kicking, Paula seemed to be effectively silenced.

In that thrashing darkness there was no telling how many of them there were. Kit took the knife in his teeth and pulled himself farther out among the lianas. A heavy loop of vine or strangler blocked him abruptly, slanting away toward the ground. Good; if it offered a quiet avenue down—

Down below, a stifled cry sounded. There was a noise of an object being dragged along the brush. Without knowing how or when it had happened, Kit realized that he was raging with desperation. He leaped for the dimly sensed loop, his hands clawed.

The instant he struck it he let go. He had made a mistake. The cold, hard cable was *alive*.

He was too late. The thick section flexed downward in a lightning response, and a screaming hiss rent the palm fronds. Kit had scarcely started to fall when coil after coil of scale-sheathed muscle lashed about his shoulders and chest.

Python!

Kit hung, every muscle limp, enswathed in the cocoon of power the big snake had dropped around him. Only his jaw muscles were clenched, to retain the knife, which was cutting cruelly into the corners of his mouth.

It would be fatal to tense even once. No amount of

strain Kit could put on his own body could match the
pressure the python could bring to bear—but if it
thought him harmless, it might let him live long enough
to work free later, somehow.

Kit waited. An itch began to crawl up his back. The
python stirred tentatively. The cold, dry hide nestled
against his cheek, and rustled over his clothing. He
could feel the snake's ribs flexing, taking a fresh grip.
The pressure was terrible, but not yet bone-breaking.

Evidently the reptile had been asleep, and had fed
recently. Though no longer in that state of torpor in
which it would abandon even self-defense in favor of
its digestion, neither was it in the excitable frame of
mind of a hunting python; it did not seem to know
whether it had caught an enemy or an impossibly over-
sized and unwelcome meal.

It moved again, flowing upward, passing Kit along
its coils as it went. The stacked loops dropped to en-
compass his legs, and cautiously he took a slow breath.
It was like fire in his lungs; until that instant he had
not realized that he had stopped breathing. Instantly
the snake halted. A moment later its head loomed directly over Kit, tongue out, tense and quivering. It was
watching—and listening. The head was black and trag-
ically stunning in silhouette.

After a while, the snake seemed satisfied. It began
to shift Kit's weight again. He felt himself being rolled
over; he guessed that he was being lashed securely to
a heavy frond.

Down below, the sounds of fighting receded and
dimmed. Then they were gone altogether. The snake
and Kit Kennedy were alone in the doum-palm.

The snake was going back to sleep. There was a
slight, pearly trace of false dawn in the air. Evidently
the creature was content to wait for another inspection,
when the light was better; it had already tested him
with its muscles, its nose, its ears, its heat-sensitive
nasal fossae, and found him curious—presumptuous
too—but not a threat. And it could wait; why not? It
had a century or so to be patient in.

"Tssssss," Kit said, softly, through the space left between the edge of the blade and the roof of his mouth.

The coils tightened—only momentarily, but in that moment Kit barely fought back his impulse to scream. The great space-shaped head wove into sight again.

"Tsssss."

The snake watched and listened, puzzled, but very certain of its own deadliness.

"Tssss."

The snake's tongue quivered and retracted. It said: *Tsssssssssss!*

The hiss was loud, but not threatening. Kit stopped breathing again. The coils shifted, very delicately.

Kit allowed himself to tense enough to regain his balance. The snake shot its tongue out again, but when Kit made no further move, it pulled its head back and allowed him to relax.

"Tsss," Kit said.

The snake began to withdraw... very slowly... very smoothly... transferring its weight to a higher branch, but—watching... listening. Years later, it was all above him, and Kit was free to clasp the frond if he dared.

He lay in precarious balance until he was satisfied that the snake was not angry. Then he opened his mouth and let the knife drop. He would have preferred to retain it, but he could feel the blood running down his chin from the split corners of his lips, and his mouth was gummed and salty.

The phython listened to the blade fall as if it were only a rotten palm cone. Kit turned cautiously, and when his erstwhile captor made no move, swung his feet down.

It would probably be fatal to try to leave, but he had very little choice. He began to work his way along the frond. The snake stirred too, and when Kit looked again, it was gone.

There was still no sign of it when he reached the ground.

It took only a moment to locate the knife again; the false dawn had disappeared, but Kit could place most sounds as accurately as a man with a map, and the knife had struck loudly. There was no longer any sign that a fight had taken place, except for a few slashed and half-collapsed tents, and a warm spot where the fire had been.

"Ktendi?"

For a second Kit froze; then the voice struck a great chord of relief in his heart.

"Tombu! Come here!"

"I am here, *bwana*."

The brush stirred, and the native beckoned from the aisle leading from the dead ashes to the moonlit grassland.

"What happened?"

"I do not know, *bwana*. Many men attacked us. I was struck on the head and left for dead; I can thank the dark for that. I think they have taken the ones who still live across the grass, perhaps to the mountain."

"There are many dead?"

"Many," Tombu said. "Soldiers and askaris. The rest—gone."

Kit thought about it. It was probable that the attack had come from a village of some size across the grassland, from whence they had heard the signals and the work drum. He doubted that it had come from as far away as the mountain; something about that stony mass suggested that a large proportion of it was still below the horizon. But then, distances were deceptive across such country. If the mountain were really an extinct volcano, as its flat top suggested, it had to be close; volcanoes in Africa were generally not old enough to reach any real height.

In any case, a party with prisoners and loot would leave a heavy spoor even trekking across veldt; and it must be close to true dawn now—there was already a faint glow over the stars.

"Pick up some canteens from among the soldiers," he said. "Full ones. We'll see if we can cross that plateau before nightfall."

"We two alone?"

"I see no one else here. Naturally the warrior Tombu is not afraid."

Tombu drew himself up. Had the statement been put as a question, he would have been mortally insulted; not even Kit could have been allowed such a taunt.

"I ask to know if I should also bring a carbine," he said with cold dignity.

Kit grinned and slapped him on the back. The African grinned and slapped him back, nearly hard enough to knock him down. This established the matter as a joke.

"Yes," Kit said. "And a bandolier."

As the man slipped away into the darkness to search the corpses, Kit felt around the base of the tree for the Davidson, sticking the knife back in his boot. Tombu, to be sure, had little taste for guns, preferring to depend upon his own black thornwood spear, a weapon with which he had grown up, his gift of princehood. Against lions, however, he was willing to carry a rifle—the tawny beasts weren't native to Gundu country, and Tombu had probably seen no more than two or three in his whole life.

As Kit straightened up, the Bantu's voice spoke softly near him.

"Do not move, *bwana*. There is trouble overhead."

Kit froze, rolling his eyes up into his head as far as he could. Depending from the cluster of fronds above him was the terrific head and about two yards of the body of the python. The neck of the beast was as big around as a man's head, at the narrowest place just behind the jaws; Kit made a lightning estimate of the length of the beast, then threw aside the result as preposterous. The snake was watching him.

Kit relaxed, insofar as he was able.

"*Ay-obwa*," he said. "His majesty of the rocks and I have a truce, I believe."

Tombu lowered his carbine dubiously.

"The big snakes move very quickly, *bwana*," he said. "And they have quick tempers. I could shoot him easily from here."

"No, don't. I have an indebtedness. Let him go."

Kit moved slowly across the little clearing toward the plateau. To his surprise, the snake did not retreat; instead, after a moment, it began to spiral down the tree-bole after him. Tombu swallowed audibly, and Kit did not feel much better himself. The creature was truly immense—not quite the thirty feet in length that Kit had initially deduced, but a good twenty-five. A small bulge about three quarters down its length suggested the almost-digested remains of some luckless shoat or kid.

Kit resumed walking; the snake followed. Kit smiled in spite of himself; there was something almost comical in so many yards of muscular, ferocious curiosity.

"All right," he said. "Come along then. I have some edible friends I'd like you to meet."

He signaled to Tombu, who moved reluctantly after him, shaking his head.

"It is as the old crones sing," the African said gravely. "'The deep jungle is the white man's grave, for only to Ktendi does the serpent tell his wisdom.'"

Kit had never heard the proverb before; it made him acutely uneasy. Things like that were not said of one in the jungle with impunity; even a man who was only *said* to talk with serpents was being offensively familiar with Father Death.

"Woman talk is seldom sensible, you know that," he said. "The long one will make up his own mind. Let's go."

He washed his mouth out from an extra canteen, shouldered a bandolier and pushed out into the chest-high grass. Tombu shrugged, looked sidelong at the python, and followed. It was, Kit reflected, a peculiar trio to be setting out against an armed and unknown village.

And perhaps against *mokele-mbemba?* Perhaps; but that did not suffer itself to be thought.

Ahead, and to the right, the sky brightened steadily, until the world was filled with steely fire from horizon to horizon. Within an hour even the water in the canvas-sheathed canteens was hot. The grass slapped at Kit's shirt, tangled his legs, crunched into choking dust at every step.

All that he might have been able to bear. What was truly intolerable was the way the veldt kept melting into a mirage of tossing wheat.

The python had vanished, but Kit's relief at this was short-lived. The low tunnels in the grass were a natural environment for it, that was all; it was still with them.

Occasionally it lifted the flat hammer of its head level with the surface of the waving brown sea, ahead of them or to one side; the unwinking black eyes would stare at Kit and Tombu; then it would be gone again.

"The long one hunts," Tombu said. Kit wished he could believe it; nothing in the behavior of the snake suggested anything so commonplace. "It will be a meager meal here."

"I've seldom seen deader-looking land," Kit agreed. "We haven't seen a mouse, let alone a lion."

He looked back at the edge of the palm forest, now noticeably on lower ground.

"We've come a long distance," he added. "But it still looks like a good trek to that mountain."

Tombu shaded his eyes.

"There is a mist between us and the cliffs. Perhaps there is a river."

"Perhaps."

It got brighter. If it also got better, Kit was beyond feeling it. Once they stopped for a few moments in the dubious shade of a dragon tree. In the baked silence Kit heard, very dimly, a pervasive sound. At first he set it down to the blood coursing through his inner ear, but when he put the butt of the Davidson to the ground the noise was perceptibly louder.

"What do you make of that, Tombu?" he said.

The native listened at the dusty turf.

"Waterfall," he said, almost at once. "A great one."

"Nonsense! In *this* country? There couldn't be a big fall that close."

"Nevertheless," Tombu said, "it is a waterfall. I have heard many and many, and I know."

Kit did not argue the matter further. When Tombu was as definite as all that, the question was settled.

"Let's push on, then. There must be a trick gorge ahead."

"I think so, *bwana*."

The plateau seemed to stretch out indefinitely. By late afternoon, however, the veil of mist had grown until the two men could no longer see it—they were in it. It cut off the blasting sun a little, but the increased humidity made the heat seem twice as bad. The sound of the invisible and impossible waterfall was quite distinct now.

"See, *bwana*," Tombu said suddenly. "The rise ahead. The edge of the gorge, beyond doubt. Already the ground is beginning to crumble."

It was inarguable. They began to climb. Within an hour they were standing on the rim.

The rim—with singular inappropriateness—of Paradise.

III *The Valley*

It was the most incredible sight that Kit had seen in twelve years of African life. He had thought himself inured to marvels, but this was beyond the marvelous; it smote the heart with all the force of a religious experience.

The plateau dropped away swiftly here, riven by a precipitous and gigantic slash like one of those valley deeps which world-girdling currents sluice out of the ocean floor. It was perhaps a mile to the bottom, or even more—the pervasive mist made the distance hard to judge. At the bottom was jungle, and the metallic flash of water. At one end, the canyon narrowed to a mere fault, through which a river rushed in boiling rapids; at the other, it wandered in a long curve north and east to the mountain.

From the face of the mountain itself a tremendous cataract arched. It seemed to issue from a tall, narrow opening in the cliff face—an underground river abruptly debouching into midair. At the base of the mountain

was a lake, at one end of which the waterfall struck in
a huge, permanent halo of fog. Over the lake, tier upon
tier, were the arches of rainbows; Kit counted seven
that seemed quite permanent, and dozens of others
flashed in and out of being constantly to the fluctua-
tions of what must have been the world's most violent
and eternal updraft.

Kit whistled softly. Tombu continued to look intently
down, his face full of wonder.

"What a monster!" Kit said softly. "It must be twice
the height of Stanley Falls."

"Yes, *bwana*, easily. I have never heard of this place."

Tombu had captured his amazement in one pithy
sentence—for surely such a place as this should be a
legend throughout the Congo, as well known to slaves
as to kings.

"This must be the source of the swamplands around
Balalondzy," Kit said. "I wonder where that river comes
out? Possibly it goes underground again."

Tombu craned his neck to the left. "I cannot see so
far, but it is likely. This valley must be cut off completely—swamps to the west, the mountain to the north
and east, and this desert of grass to the south. Even
demons might live in peace here."

Kit pricked up his ears. The word Tombu had used
meant "demons," but it also meant "night shapes," an
altogether more dubious class of entity than the man-
ifold evil spirits whose malice must be forever placated
by *juju*. Kit was very far from understanding the mul-
tifoliate faith of the Bantus—he had long ago developed
the good sense to trust a certain shaman in such matters—but he had managed to grasp at least roughly
the heirarchy of the spirits: what Tombu meant here
was not that class of devils which exists to capture and
feed on a man's soul, nor whose shadowless spiteful
mindless influences—so subtly and terrifyingly like
vagrant emotions—which are the ghosts of the im-
properly buried dead, but instead a group of shapes
which a European might have called elementals—the
embodied savage facts of jungle life and death, of which
a crocodile or a lion is only an echo. One of these, for
instance, is the Lust-to-Devour; it is real, and such crea-

tures as the driver ants—the *bafumba*—are only fractionally real beside it, their very name only a Bantu word for an itch, though it strip to the bone.

These are the night shapes. *Mokele-mbemba* was one.

It was hard to think that such a thing could be so of a valley like this, an enclave in savagery which might well have been created after the model of that garden planted eastward in Eden...*And a river went out of Eden to water the garden; and from thence it was parted, and became into four heads. The name of the first is Pison: that is it which compasseth the whole land of Havilah, where there is gold; and the gold of that land is good: there is bdellium and the onyx stone. And the name of the second river is Gihon: the same is it that compasseth the whole land of Ethiopa....*

The bony head of the python slid into Kit's field of view and glided to a stop, some distance away and to the left where the valley began to turn toward the cleft. The great reptile looked over the brim of the gorge for a long time. Then it began to move west, its body emerging sinuously and beautifully from the grasses. Evidently it had done with them at last.

"Manalendi will know the way down," Tombu said, pointing after it. "It occurs to me that he lives there. If we were trekking toward his house, he would be disturbed and would follow. A smaller snake would have gone the wrong way instead."

It was like a flash of sheet lightning in the densest midnight. "Of course!" Kit said softly. "But we couldn't have guessed that until now. Follow him, Tombu."

"That is not wise, Ktendi."

"I know it. But he isn't angry with us yet. And I want to stay off the path men travel. That would be still more unwise."

Tombu did not answer. He slid over the edge of the gorge and began to work his way west after the python, using his spear expertly for an alpenstock.

It was a long and tortuous route the python took, deceptively easy to the eye, but mostly unfit for men to travel; they had to give it up before they were a quarter of the way down, when the twilight made it increasingly impossible to judge even small distances. They spent the night on a furze-tangled ledge, sitting back to back—not as watchmen, for they were each convinced that nothing but scorpions could attack them here, but each to prevent the other from toppling sideways down the steep slope as sleep stole upon him.

The morning came upon them like the ague of breakbone fever; they lost a precious hour waiting for the slow sun to bake the stiffness out of them, while they munched somnolently on bark-tough smoked antelope venison.

Part of the bone-deep malaise seemed to have been pounded in by the drum, which had begun its regular, meaningless thumping at dusk, plainly audible even at this height through the droning, pounding roar of the waterfall. Even on a featherbed no one can sleep soundly to a nightlong command to *work, work; work, work; work, work*...

But at last they were ready to begin their long slither into the vast garden. By midday the air was much thicker and full of moisture, and the undergrowth was beginning to luxuriate into the familiar tangle of the rain forest, offering plenty of cover. By unspoken agreement, they continued to work west. If there was a village in the valley—and plainly there was—it had to be situated where the river was choked into rapids; any other situation would be indefensible.

By the time they reached the bottom, it was late afternoon again; but they were once more in terrain thrice-familiar, however new: the eternal jungle.

"Manalendi is gone," Tombu said.

"I'm just as well pleased. He's probably getting hungry."

Tombu turned and looked at Kit with a curiously flat, questioning expression.

"You did not bind him?"

"No," Kit said. He did not know how otherwise to answer the question. It was possible to bind serpents; Kit did not sneer at *juju*, he had seen too much of it. But by the same token he knew equally well that he had none of his own, for to command spirits takes a lifetime of study—there are charlatans even among

witch doctors. Once Kit had seen once such man die,
and that had cured him of any residual urges to play
the white magician, even when it might have been most
to his immediate advantage.

"Snakes are curious, you know that," he said halt-
ingly. "And Manalendi saw that we were going toward
his home—you saw that. I cannot bind, Tombu. I am
not a sorcerer."

"True," Tombu said. "But you are a king. All the
great and little gods love kings. I tell you so. And Manalendi is a king: see."

He pointed. A river of multicolored prisms was passing through the very tops of the trees just over them.
The python was there, as restless as an ancient and
troubling thought which could not quite be put into
words. Probably it was hungry, probably it was hunting, probably it was disturbed, probably it was curious... probably, probably; but there, in fact, it was.

Very well, Kit thought grimly, let the thing follow
us. It may have its uses later. But he was shaken, all
the same.

"Let's locate those drummers," he said. "It'll be night
again very shortly. We have to know where the village
is. And find the fat white man, the rifle white man, the
doctor, the white woman. Otherwise they may be eaten."

"That is possible," Tombu murmured. His own tribe
had not been particular about long pig before the blood
pact between Tombu and Kit; now and again they still
popped a prisoner on a spit while Kit was away. But
only in the knowledge that Ktendi would know; somehow, he always knew; he had the gift of sight, unlike
white men.

"There are little drums there," Tombu said after a
moment. "It cannot be far, by the sound."

They worked their way cautiously among the boabab
trees. The going was thick for a while; and then, suddenly, there was no more going at all: a tree lay fallen
squarely in front of them. The giant trunk must have
taken more than a century to form; it seemed to have
fallen when its weight became too great even for its

vast root system to support in the spongy ground. Since
then it had become overgrown. It would have taken
days to cut a path around it; it took an hour to climb.

On the other side, the drums were louder; and to a
vagrant shift in the wind, a terrific stench rolled down
upon them, rather like the smell in the swamps of the
marshes, but worse, incredibly worse.

"Great God in Heaven," Kit whispered. "The place
smells six weeks dead. Is that just swamp, Tombu?"

"No, *bwana*. It is as you say: *makili mingi,* there is
much blood. I do not understand."

"Nor I. That can be no ordinary epidemic. I thought
we might hole up and sleep an hour or so after we found
the *kraal,* if there was nothing we had to do at once.
But not in that stink!"

Tombu's sense of humor was rudimentary; though
he often laughed, he made jokes of his own seldom more
than once a year. He made one now:

"Ibwa wete joi ja nkakamwa, bondele," he said solemnly. "Death is strange; here we should throw away
the guns, and carry brooms."

Kit said quietly:

"I am going to carry a gun in there, Tombu. And I'm
coming out with the Lees and Herr Stahl. I have plans
for all of them."

"That is fitting for a king," Tombu said, instantly
serious. He nodded to the left. "There is the clearing,
Ktendi; they hide behind the fallen tree. Let us make
them dead."

They crept closer. In a moment, they saw the village.
It was not as large as Kit had expected. It was sur-
rounded by the usual thorn *boma,* but on this side it
was in bad repair; evidently the tribe had no reason to
fear any attack from the purlieu of the fallen tree. On
the other side, however—the side toward the river—
there was a heavily reinforced palisade so tall that Kit
could see its sharpened stake tops even from this bad
a vantage point; those stakes were tree trunks which
must have taken generations to drive. He had never
before seen anything in black Africa so suggestive of
furious determination prolonged through what must
have been nearly the whole of history of the tribe, each

vast stake as firm a tribute to time as the begats in
Genesis, or the stones of the ruined fortresses of Ethio-
pia. No tribe in the Congo had ever built such a structure... until this one, which must have been free of the
slave raids of any possible neighbors far back into its
oral prehistory.

Inside, the small drums were making a melody, as
though the witch doctor were telling some secret story
to the young men on the night before circumcision. Over
them the work drum throbbed and throbbed, slowly
becoming louder, and occasionally there was a sound
like the cracking of a whip. The singing drums died;
perhaps they had not been singing to the young men,
but to the girls; if so, now the old man had to leave the
skins and go to enlarge the genitals of the maidens with
his withered mouth, before the small lips and the cli-
toris went under the knife. The big drum went on: *Work,
work; work, work; work, work...*

All that was normal, except for the continuation of
the work pulse into the night—but *mnai djuna,* the
smell! The wind had changed again, but it could not
carry away that appalling odor even from this distance.
The miasma dissolved the specter of Paradise that Kit
had imagined himself seeing from the rim of the valley;
here as everywhere in the Congo, God the Creator is
good, and hence is paying no attention to what happens
in the savannahs of his imagination; down there rule
the creatures of evil in whom God the Creator, who is
good, cannot bring himself to believe. *Mnai djuna*—
foul things, do not touch me!

"I want to see what that structure is on the other
side of the village," Kit said softly. "I'll have to climb
for it. I don't see why they shouldn't even need a *poshi*
on this side, and want a fortress on the other. You'd
best stay down here and keep an eye out, just in case."

Tombu nodded, and Kit picked out a likely-looking
tree. As he climbed, the odor changed; it did not become
either less or more intense, but it became easier to
separate out some of its components. Rancid shea butter
was certainly one; blood just as certainly another.

In the foliage ahead of him, what appeared to be a
thick branch stirred gently and began to flow away from

him. Then a triangular head butted through a dense tangle of lianas and stared down at him: Manalendi, his majesty of the rocks, was back again. Kit stared back warily for a moment, and then said softly:

"Tss. Upstairs, handsome."

The Long One flicked his tongue out and back and withdrew his head. The "branch" began to flow again. As Kit resumed climbing, he became aware that the snake was climbing too, not ahead of him exactly, but all around him, like some dynamic cocoon. Had Manalendi adopted him as a pet? The notion was ridiculous, but nobody could know what went on in the mind of a python; it had no natural enemies, and when it was not either hungry or torpidly fed, it was free to indulge whatever notions crept into its cold, fist-sized brain.

Whatever was animating it at the moment, it was a nuisance, for it made climbing very difficult. Kit did not flatter himself that Manalendi had made friends with him; were he to lay a demanding hand on the snake by mistake, it might well lose its patience with him on the spot, and drop him at Tombu's feet with most of his bones scientifically broken into splinters. The creature was curious, and the curiosity had proved unnaturally long lasting—but the thread of its neutrality could be snapped by the smallest insult to its integrity.

After a while, nevertheless, Kit judged that he was high enough. He tried to peer down while he rested; maddeningly, he could see quite a sizable patch of dark turf, but not the patch where Tombu was standing. If the African could still see him, he must have climbed the fallen tree—which, Kit realized, was sensible, for it would give Tombu a better view of the top of the boma as well, and hence enable him to give the alarm more quickly if a *poshi* should appear along the tops of the thornwood stakes.

He wriggled forward and parted the bunched leaves to look downward into the *kraal*. After a moment, the greenery just next to him rustled. He could not see what had caused the motion, but he suspected that Manalendi was now watching too.

The village below was larger than he had first judged

it to be. Inside the decayed boma the huts were well
made, and the lodges of chieftain and wizard were both
large and well-decorated with colored mud, chalk,
feathers, and human knuckle-bone jewelry. There was
a sizable skull rack beside the central clearing, with
heads plentiful upon it—so plentiful that the poorer
specimens had simply been cast upon a great heap just
outside the firelight.

There was another heap squarely before the chief's
lodge, but it was not skulls, nor anything else that Kit
could recognize. Possibly it was peat, though the fires
did not seem big enough to demand so much reserve
fuel. Yet it was growing bigger all the time. A sham-
bling procession of natives was adding to it, carrying
more of the unidentifiable substance from the direction
of the river. A small figure standing on a low platform
near the pile seemed to be directing the work; brawny,
tattoo-scarred tribesmen paced along the files with
heavy whips.

The laden figures—slaves, that went without saying, but sick slaves too, from the way they stumbled
and moaned—were coming in from the wall on the river
side of the village. They came in singly, through an
opening barely large enough to allow them to pass
through bent double under their burdens, and they came
through in a hurry, like men who would rather be under
the whips of their overseers than out there in the river-
murmuring twilight beyond the wall. The slaves who
waited their turn to slip out that same hole, after each
laden man lurched in, cringed as though their terror
was a greater burden to them than whatever they would
be asked to carry later. The whips cracked more often
over them than over the slaves inside, though the pace
set by the incessantly hammering work drum was cruel
beyond belief.

The structure on the river side was a wall, no more
than that: a wall built as a barricade against giants,
and braced to withstand cannon, or even earthquakes.
Now that Kit could see all of it, it made even less sense
to him than it had when he could see only its top. There
was a catwalk of vines suspended just inside the sharpened tops of the trees, and huge, smoking torches were

fixed regularly all along the walk; beside each torch was a warrior, his back turned to the town, his eyes bent on the incipient darkness outside, watching for—what?

Kit's eyes roved, searching for clues. There were none. This was the place he had been searching for, all the same, for he could see some of his boys and two Belgian soldiers hung by their heels in back of the skull rack, neatly butchered and ready for curing; over one of the fires an enormous iron kettle, full to the brim with black water, bubbled gently, loosening another man's skin for subsequent flaying; and another fire burned fiercely in a deep trench, where the gutted corpse, sprinkled with salt crystals and stuffed and wrapped with plantain leaves, would be roasted to a delicate turn no later than tomorrow night.

There was no sign of the Lees, Stahl or van Bleyswijck, and darkness was coming closer with every moment; when night fell in this valley, it would close down with abrupt finality. The village went on with its obscure business, as though indifferent to the imminent night. To Kit's left, there was a stir of departure: Manalendi—bored at last. Kit could sympathize; his own brain was foggy with fatigue. Tombu, though he had not complained, was probably nearly as tired. Surely tomorrow would be soon enough to—

Suddenly, the drums changed their tune. A rattle of little gourds went up, a pittering of monkey hide, the bony clatter of a xylophone. The big council drum began to pulse excitedly. Torches were lit. Someone was whining away at a water flute.

The whips cracked, and the slaves dumped their loads upon the hoard and were herded away, wailing with hopeless weariness. The music got louder.

Kit clung and listened, fascinated. The many musics of Africa affected him deeply, and he had never heard any more exciting than this. There was a feral eagerness in it, a surcharge of blood lust, a terrible undercurrent of raw power—and a strange, scalp-prickling note of fear, fear of something beyond all human experience. Nor could he be in any real doubt about these meanings, for in a culture using an intoned language, melody always has a semantic content denied to the music of Europe.

There was going to be a *ngoma* in the village; but the celebration it promised would be half delirium and half death.

The sunset went out in a blast of color, and there was no longer any light at all but the flaring of the torches. Kit cautiously worked his way back, making as much allowance as he could for how tired he was, and inched his way down the trunk.

"Tombu?"

"*Awa,* Ktendi. *Wapi ye?*"

"The snake? He's either finally given us up, or bedded himself down somewhere aloft. No matter. We've got to get in there at once. They're cooking up some sort of deviltry."

Tombu said, "I hear them. There will be more blood soon, I think. I know that song; it is the song of *jilo,* the manhunger."

"Ah." That explained a good deal. The strange tribe was about to have a feast—upon its captives, of course—to celebrate its victory, and the gaining of so many *bondoki* and other firearms.

Probably some of the prisoners were still alive, and the intention would be to keep them alive for later— meat being more precious than gold in acid-soiled Africa. But it would be foolish to trust in that intention. Once a *ngoma* was in full swing no man could predict the turns it might take; this was what Tombu had meant.

"All right, Tombu. Let us make them dead."

IV *The River*

In the fitful glow from the village, the jungle was unearthly, with shadows distorting everything, and creating movement where there was nothing to move. Even at night the ground steamed. Enormous orchids clung like spiders to clumps of moss on the trees. The lianas bore milk-white flowers, unfamiliar to Kit yet uneasily suggestive; he could not think of what. The cables of the convolvuli were sometimes as thick as his wrist, and rearing amid the tangle of brush were the calcified spines of tree ferns and giant horsetail; Kit had never seen either before, and he was hard put to it to be certain he was not dreaming. Tombu's brush knife glimmered in the feeble torchlight.

There was a gate in the southwest side of the boma, closed, but apparently unwatched. The two men skirted it, taking to the trees to cross the well-beaten trail which led away from it. Kit pointed to a cluster of hut roofs farther along the line.

"Those have all the earmarks of slave quarters," he

muttered. "And unless I'm way off, that's where the stink is coming from."

Tombu nodded. "So it would seem, *bondele*. There are two guards posted by the little one, the one nearest the boma."

"Yes—that's probably where the white woman and the others are. I find it odd that they leave the other slaves unguarded."

"Where would they go?"

"Mmm. I see. It's that they can't trust the whites to know better; is that it?"

"Bendele bafa banto."

"You know, Tombu, that isn't really true. But it covers the situation, evidently. All right, we'll work in toward the wall there, then. I think we can cut our way into that hut from behind."

Tombu swung off the branch and clambered with the certainty of a monkey down the tangle of vines by the wall. Kit followed, a little hampered by his boots and the heavy smoothbore, but oddly, no longer aware that he was tired. They dropped almost soundlessly to the ground in the shadow of the wall.

Gingerly, Tombu worked his knife into a crack of dim light. The boma stakes were still strong and pliant, but the interwoven vines evidently were old and brittle. They split with an electrical crackling which seemed loud as thunder to Kit, but the music inside went on without even slackening. After another moment Tombu stepped aside.

Kit passed him the Davidson, slipped his shoulder into the breach and forced himself cautiously through. He put his ear to the corrugated back wall of the hut.

Inside, familiar voices murmured: Paula's, Stahl's. He could not make out the words, but at least they were still alive; that was a start. He plucked the knife from his boot and shredded the poles with quick strokes.

"What's that?" Paula whispered sharply.

Kit pushed into the hut. "Shh," he said. "I don't want a welcoming committee."

"It's Kit Kennedy," the girl breathed, and the words were like a prayer. "I thought they'd killed you!"

"A sensible assumption, but I'm happy to prove it wrong. How many of you are there in this stink hole?"

"Just we two," Stahl's voice said in the dense blackness. "They have van Bleyswijck and Howard somewhere else, unless they are already dead."

"Probably not," Kit said. He padded to the door and peered through a slit in the stiff hide. The celebration was going on unabated, as the sounds had already told him. One of the guards was nodding, the other one watching the dancers. Kit grunted and came back.

"They won't start on you two and the others until tomorrow night, if I'm any judge. For the moment they've got more meat than they can handle."

"They'll—eat us?" Paula whispered.

"Certainly. It's normal and natural. This whole continent is protein-poor, and there's too much animal competition for what game there is. Meat is meat. But you've got a little while. There's a drum as big as a hippo in the compound—the one the overseer was standing on, if you saw her—so there'll probably be a drum duel tomorrow."

"What's that?" Stahl said stolidly. If the prospect of being eaten disturbed him, it did not show in his voice.

"That," Kit said grimly, "is something that doesn't concern you, for which you ought to be thankful. Now speak up. I want to know what this safari was all about, or you'll go under the knife with my blessing. I'm sick of all this mystery, and I swear I'll leave you both here for good unless you give me the whole story."

There was a brief silence.

"All right," Stahl said, rather glumly. Kit could almost see him shrugging. "These people are mining pitchblende."

"Pitchblende? Is that radium ore?"

"Yes. The Congo is very rich in it, as you may know—as one would expect of any country where there is also gold. They tend to occur together."

"I didn't know that. Go on."

"Quite a lot of it was appearing on the market that hadn't left the colony legally. It had all the characteristics of Congo ore, but it was way above the Belgian quota. The material is deadly to handle unless one is very careful; so when we received reports that there was a leprosylike disease raging up near Balalondzy, we drew the logical conclusion."

"And since nobody would go on digging pitchblende of his own free will—not after he'd seen what it could do—the Reform Committee smelled slavery and sent me along to investigate," Paula added.

"I see," Kit said thoughtfully. "Then the stench around here really does represent the death rate—and of course nobody eats sick prisoners; hence acute cannibalism in the midst of apparent plenty. Fascinating! Everything in Africa is unique."

"I can't be quite so detached," Stahl said. "In any event we brought only a small military force, because we knew that if the ore was leaving the country illegally, the traffic had to have the cooperation of a white man somewhere along the line. If we'd sent a really adequate expedition, we might have broken up the traffic and the slavery, but the head man—I was sure *you* were that man, Kennedy—would escape with all his loot and be free to re-establish himself in some new venture. What I wanted was to cut us off and make our position look harmless, indeed virtually hopeless, so that the real leaders wouldn't be afraid to reveal themselves to us."

Stahl's brief groan was almost comical.

"I didn't expect to succeed so well," he finished. "Here we are as good as dead already, and I *still* have no idea who is in back of this death camp."

"I may be able to tell you," Kit said. "But not unless you're willing to stay here a while longer to establish it. I'm taking Paula with me the way I came in, so if you'd rather not take the risk—"

"I'll stay," Stahl said resignedly. "I cannot very well abandon van Bleyswijck if he still lives; and besides, my assignment is not complete."

Kit felt a surge of admiration. Never before in his whole career had he had a man so thoroughly wrong.

"Good," he said. "Paula, let's—"

"I'm staying too," Paula announced evenly.

"You're out of your mind!" Kit swallowed and started again. "I'm sorry, Paula, but my chances of getting Stahl and your husband out of here before it's too late are about one in ninety. If there are two of you, it'll be absolutely impossible."

"I understand that," the girl said calmly. "But if you and Tombu have to be worrying about taking care of me while you're working—well, you'll be handicapped. Besides, if the tribesmen find Otto still here and me gone, they'll post so many guards you won't be able to do *anything*."

She sounded dead sure of herself. Kit scratched his head. What she said made sense, furthermore. How did you deal with a logical woman? There weren't supposed to be any such.

Stahl started, "Paula, it's absurd for you—"

She cut in, with a voice like the edge of a knife, "I don't want to be killed, and I won't be an impediment to my own rescue."

"All right," Kit said at last. "God knows you've got nerve, Paula. Sit tight, both of you, and don't panic. I'll get you out, somehow."

He pushed back out to the break in the *boma.*

He felt like a man who had just promised someone the moon.

Outside, Tombu was waiting, motionless and silent. Here the sound of the music was subdued, and more than a little masked by the pervasive roar of the nearby waterfall. Kit listened a moment.

"There is much work," he said at last. "But I'm still not satisfied. There's more that needs to be known. Go back to the fallen tree, Tombu, I'll meet you there later."

"Where will I look if you do not come, *bondela?*"

"Nowhere; go home in that case. I want to look at that river."

Tombu melted away. Kit worked his way along the perimeter of the *boma,* until the smell of water told him that he must be nearing the river gate; then he angled off into the jungle, guiding himself as best he could by the loudness of the falls.

He struck the river shore abruptly. The jungle did not stop, but marched on into the shallow; he was already up to his knees. There was some moonlight here, and the torches atop the walls made wavering lines of yellow on the swift, oily-looking water.

The falls themselves were hidden by a turn in the gorge, but on the far wall he saw something else: a huge natural arch in the cliff face, almost fifty feet high, fronted by an artificial clearing. That, undoubtedly, was the mine.

The water in his boots reminded him that he had not had them off his feet for a long time; since before the attack on the plateau, in fact. He retreated into the jungle and stripped himself of everything but his knife, spreading his clothes out on the scaly bark of a squat, huge doum-palm, and then found himself a relatively clear inlet to bathe in.

He was quick about it; but just before he had finished, there was a sound downstream as of some large body breaking the surface. He parted the reeds and peered intently.

But he could see very little. There was something large in midstream, that was certain, something large and black, with the moonlight making a line of cold light along its wet back. It might have been a hippo, except that it was a little too big for that, and it seemed to have a very large head; but he knew better than to trust any impression that his eyes formed in this dimness.

Then, suddenly, it made a sound: *Hhhouchgh!* It was half cough and half roar, with a hissing edge to it. Not a hippo sound, or indeed any sound that he had ever heard before. He stood stock still, watching the thing turn its massive ambiguous head from side to side in the water.

Finally, it disappeared. It did not dive, but simply sank, until there was nothing left of it. Kit waited until he could be certain that it was not going to surface near to him, though he was fairly sure that there was no real danger of that—the animal obviously had been going slowly downstream, away from him and the falls.

Then he climbed out of the shallows, pausing only to pull the leeches off his ankles, and dressed in a hurry. The water flute whined sleepily, and the drumming

sounded thin and mechanical. Kit stirred in the crotch
of the big shea tree.

"Tombu?"

"Yes, *bwana.*"

"A few questions, and I'll let you sleep."

The African sat part way up. A vagrant ray of moonlight shimmered along his bare arm.

"First of all—during the attack back there in the
palm forest, did you hear a woman's voice?"

"Only at the beginning, calling 'Attack, attack!'"
Tombu said.

"That's right. And that was a woman on the drum,
the big drum, driving the slaves when we first looked
in the *kraal.*"

"Yes."

"A white woman?"

"I do not know. She was dressed like an Arab; I could
not see her skin. But African women do not give orders."

"Precisely." Kit shifted, scratching his back against
the tree-bole. There were only a few hours left in which
to make up two days' sleep, but he had to know where
the weak spots in this tangled net might be.

"All right. Now. We know what that big drum is
for—you don't strike a death drum often. But where
did you last see a wall like that one near the river?"

"At Notama," the native said. "On the Ssombo.
Though that one is not so tall and strong. The same
vine grows there, too, *bondela*—the liana with the white
flowers and sweet fruit."

"Yes, I saw the flowers. I will tell you else: I think
I have seen the creature himself."

"Tonight, *bondela?*"

"Yes. The forest legends are not often wrong, are
they, Tombu?"

"No, *bondela;* not often."

"All right," Kit said. "We'll act accordingly. There's
no way to get a message out of here except with the big
drum, so we'll have to use it. I'll need a simple word,
one that I can repeat over and over; one that comes in
a short tune. What shall I use?"

Tombu thought. "I am not a *girot,*" he said. "I am a
king."

"I know it well, Tombu, or I'd not have asked. To a king all things are possible."

"I would use *yo*," Tombu said. "The tune is, *Awa yo bafumba adjali*, but *awa yo* is sufficient for a summons."

Awa yo bafumba adjali: There is evil here, with the word for "driver ants" acting as an intensifier, as one might say "teeming" in English but with far more urgency. If any of the Wassabi heard that, it would undoubtedly bring them. *If* they heard it.

"Good; I thank you. We'd better get some sleep now— we'll need it."

Tombu grunted and settled back again. Kit closed his eyes. It was the first chance he had had to really think about what would be happening to Paula in the prisoners' hut and it filled him with cold fury—which rather surprised him, but after all it had happened already and could not be undone; and Paula had been, apparently, prepared for it. As for the rest, once he had his course of action planned, he wasted no energy worrying over whether or not it would work. A man who worries has time for nothing else in the jungle. Shortly, he slept.

The work drum thudded brainlessly all through the stifling day, but at sundown the rattle and clamor of the celebration began again. A huge fire was built in the center of the village. This time the slaves were not driven back into their foul huts, but were herded into an arc and seated, shoulder to shoulder, at the back of the clearing near the skull rack.

Kit watched the procedure grimly. Those poor animals weren't being brought in to serve as an audience, that was certain. It was more likely that they were intended as raw material for the forthcoming ceremony. He beckoned to Tombu.

"Time to go," he said.

The African nodded, swung out over the limb and dropped, Kit close on his heels. The gate in the *boma* was still closed and apparently unguarded, and the two men walked boldly toward it. Above them, there was a sudden, agitated rustling of leaves; a moment later, and

Manalendi was gliding beside them, leaving a sinuous trail in the dust.

"That's a break," Kit said softly. "I thought he'd gone away for good. What does he think he's doing, I wonder?"

Tombu paused by the gate and made a trumpet of his hands.

"Mbote!" he bellowed. "Open, open! Open for Ktendi, prince of all the Gundu warriors! Open for Tombu, mighty chieftan and hunter! Open for Manalendi, eldest son of Wisdom!"

Kit suppressed a grin. Good manners in the jungle made no virtue of modesty, of course; but the touch about the snake was unexpectedly imaginative of Tombu.

The black king thundered again, his tremendous voice rolling out over the frenetic music. The sounds inside faltered and lessened. Then the *boma* creaked to the pounding of feet running along its inner platform, and a moment later at least ten spearmen were looking down upon them. Their eyes bulged as they saw the python.

"We come in peace," Tombu called, spreading his fingers. "We would speak with the king of this mighty nation."

One of the tribesmen jumped down into the village. The others simply watched, spears poised. Finally they were joined by a tremendous man, at least as big as Tombu; his brawny black body was elaborately striped with white clay, and over his head he wore a ceremonial mask. His arms were brilliant with scarlet flamingo feathers and brass bracelets; obviously he had been interrupted in some ritual observance.

"Endoka tofa la bonyolo," he boomed. "I am N'mbono. I am chief of all the forest people from the mountain to the swamps, lord of the river and the falls, and high priest to Nanan and the Rock God."

Again Kit could hardly repress a sour grin. N'mbono's traditional greeting, "Here we have no chain to bind you," did not comport very well with what Kit already knew went on behind those walls; but then, the chief would have been astonished to have been taken literally.

"*Baminga,* great king," he said, pointing to heaven and to his heart. "Your fame has spread even until the lodges of the Gundu tribes, and your wisdom is whispered among the serpents." He turned and addressed a few meaningless noises to Manalendi, who had arranged himself in two separate piles of coils, as though his latter half were not governed by the same brain as his front half, just before the gate, and was staring directly at the mask of N'mbono. "We have come in peace, as brother chiefs, to compete in the games of which the drums have chanted."

Evidently this calm announcement took N'mbono aback. It seemed likely that he knew that Kit and Tombu had been part of the safari before it had been captured—yet here they were, effectively offering to give themselves up! It was not reasonable, and therefore dangerous. Besides, the reports of N'mbono's warriors could have said nothing about a huge and unpleasantly single-minded-looking python.

"You ask that which is death," he said finally. "Go away as you came, or be welcomed by the wrath of Nanan and the Rock God."

"He's playing safe," Kit said swiftly in French. "Wouldn't turn down fresh meat otherwise. A little more brass, Tombu." Then, to N'mbono:

"We fear no gods not our own. Who dies in the games, dies of weak arms and faint heart. It is widely sung that N'mbono is strong and courageous. Shall I tell the Gundu and the Wassabi tribes that the tale-bearers lie?"

The feathers on N'mbono's arms quivered angrily. Kit was in some doubt as to whether he would admit them or order his spearmen to slay them on the spot, but he never found out what the chief might have done. Manalendi, bored with all this standing around and intent upon his own unfathomable purposes, stirred and reared swiftly toward the top of the *boma.*

The warriors scattered and jumped in panic. N'mbono stood his ground for a moment longer, then disappeared after the rest. The snake peered after them, as if baffled by all this meaningless activity, and then began to subside.

Kit marched forward and pushed open the gate.

There was a long, fairly broad path directly to the big fire, but it was enfilated on both sides by the dark alleys between the mud-and-thatch huts. Kit forced himself to walk slowly. N'mbono had lost *mpifo* before his warriors, and there was a fifty-fifty chance that he would not have them ambushed; if they could once reach the central clearing...

As they came closer, something new became visible on the other side of the leaping flames: a huge, crude throne, carved out of soft stone, and a small figure sitting motionless upon it. Kit looked straight ahead and kept walking, Tombu to his right. The music was completely silent now, and as the duo came into the firelight, an awed murmur went up among the assembled warriors. Kit studied their eyes, and concluded that Manalendi was not far behind.

The figure on the throne rose slowly. It was the woman Kit had seen from the tree outside—doubtless the same one who had spurred the attack upon the encampment. Not greatly to his surprise, she was not a black woman, but an Asiatic or Semitic type. She looked hard as iron, and not young anymore, but her figure fitted Kit's theories well enough.

She was clad in a single, clinging robe, a dirty white abaiyia which left her olive arms and shoulders bare, caught together at the waist with a tremendous gold clasp in the shape of an animal's head—a head a little like a rhino's, and yet not very like a rhino's either. Her hair was coal-black, and wound into a bizarre coronal; her eyes, too, were black, and glowing with a passionate, cruel vitality.

This, then, was the woman N'mbono had called Nanan; a French name, but hardly a European woman; more likely the product of some stew of Port Said or Dar-es-Salaam. She had the key, if she could be persuaded to give it up. Kit was far from confident that she would be so foolish.

"Who is this trespasser?" she cried in a ringing, sing-

song voice. "Who walks in the circle sanctified by the
Rock God?"

Kit stopped and made the three signs of peace once
more. Since the mask of N'mbono was now beside her
throne, she must know very well who he was, but the
forms had to be observed.

"I," he said, "am Ktendi."

The circle of warriors remained silent, but from the
massed prisoners there came a fluttering of excitement.
A whip cracked warningly. Kit's prestige was obviously
of little account here, for the isolated village could hardly
have heard much about him; but the slaves, almost all
of them from outside the valley, knew the name and
whispered it—not in hope, for that would be insane,
but simply in wonder at a new thing come into their
lives since yesterday.

"You are a *bendele*," Nanan said. "You bear a Bantu
name, but you are not of the people. We spit on such
playacting."

She sat down once again. "Bring the other captives,
that this one who calls himself Ktendi may see how we
respect the whites."

N'mbono stepped away from the throne into the
darkness.

"I know of these captives," Kit said sternly. "And I
tell you that great evil is being done here. The gods of
my country mean that it shall end."

"The gods of your country?" Nanan touched the gold
clasp and laughed. "Kind little gods, and harmless. The
Rock God has the power in this place. He is strange
and terrible. He takes all forms that are pleasing to
him, and commands all the lesser gods and demons.
Those whom he smites die slowly."

The mask of N'mbono, like a grotesque balloon,
drifted into the firelight again. With him were five
guards, and three familiar figures: Paula, Stahl, and
the marine. Van Bleyswijck seemed to be in fairly good
shape, but Stahl was blinking and haggard, and so was
the girl. Evidently they had been kept in the dark hut
all during the day. There was no sign of Howard Lee.
After a quick glance, Kit kept his gaze straight ahead.

"The Rock God is known to me," he said. "He has no

shape. He sleeps in the cliffs, and smites none who disturb him not. He has slept long and long with the gold behind pitchblende, and makes honest men richer for their honesty. Those who drive slaves have a different ending."

"That," Nanan said, "is a lie."

"Ktendi never lies," Tombu said. "He is a prince."

N'mbono said unexpectedly to Tombu: "The Rock God has made the nation of N'mbono rich, aye, and powerful. This your Ktendi may be a prince, and it is seen that he commands serpents, which is strong *juju*. But the Rock God commands *mokele-mbemba*."

A hiss of indrawn breath came from Tombu, but Kit did not blink an eyelash. He was morally certain that Tombu's surprise had been for effect; for after all, what else had they been talking about in the shea tree?

"A fable for children," he said, his voice dripping with contempt. "Those who command that Father of Night Shapes have no need for high walls. Forbear that boast, *nibo*, or he will come for you—and no one will be left to wail for your nation."

"Enough!" the northern woman cried, springing up. "This one denies the god and his priestess, and speaks spells in the name of peace! Kill him!"

"Tsssss," Kit said. The woman drew back, startled.

Manalendi's head glided into Kit's cone of vision and reared back, shot straight up into the air, six feet, eight feet, ten. Its tongue quivered alarmingly; Kit's sudden sharp call had startled it, perhaps even frightened it. The circle of warriors took one dubious step closer and then halted. In a moment, perhaps, Nanan or N'mbono would be able to pitch them up to attacking despite the python, but for the instant, Kit had the advantage. He knew very well that he did not deserve it; until now, he could not even have been certain that the snake was still behind him. He jumped into the breach before it should vanish.

"Does the great N'mbono fear for his life?" he sang out. "See how he orders his warriors to certain death in the coils of the son of Wisdom—while the great drum is bare of dancers!"

The warriors looked at N'mbono, astonished. Unless

this tribe was impossibly different from others which practiced the drum duel, they were accustomed to selecting the drum's victims from among prisoners. A man who challenged the king to the drum of his own free will could have only one purpose in mind: to become king himself. *Bendele* or no, this Ktendi must be already a king in some other place, to have such a madness at all.

"N'mbono fears nothing," the warrior rumbled. "He will meet the white stranger on the drum."

"Kit!" Paula cried. "Kit—"

There was an outburst of whispering among the slaves and the whip cracked viciously. Instead of silencing them, however, it produced a low, concerted growl of anger. Ktendi's arrival had done wonderful things for their morale, that was plain. The foremen let the whip trail. He was evidently well aware of how far he dared go with slaves in this temper.

Nanan said: "The white stranger is the appointed sacrifice to the Rock God. It is not meet that he die by the hand of battle."

"N'mbono will meet him on the drum," the warrior said. *"Kosala pila moko ngai koloba."*

Nanan's lips thinned, but she said nothing more. A challenge was serious business; she could not interfere on behalf of her headman without confessing weakness.

Manalendi, seeing that no special excitement was forthcoming, coiled up again, but kept his head erect, darting his tongue in and out nervously. The warriors made a wide circle around him to prepare the drum.

M'mbono removed his mask, revealing a round, hairless head and the heavy, confident, ruthless features of a man long accustomed to the exercise and privileges of power. Several of his wives came forward to strip him down of his feathers and finery.

Kit knelt and unlaced his boots deliberately, then took off his shirt, boots and puttees. He looked quickly over to the prisoners. Their faces were very white, especially Paula's. With sudden decision he strode over toward them.

As he approached, the *poshi* crossed their spears in front of him, but he was close enough now. At this

distance the odor from among the slaves was almost
unbearable, and he scanned the close-set ranks curiously.

It was the first time he had gotten a clear look at
the slaves of the Rock God, and even his steel-walled
stomach rebelled at what he saw. To the last man they
looked as if they had been gnawed by rats. Some were
in worse condition than others, but all were stippled
everywhere with lumpy petachiae, and painted with
bruises of that peculiar rainbow coloration which sig-
nifies an injury of long standing. Most had ulcerous
sores on their limbs and faces. Many had only a part
of their faces left, like the lion-face of leprosy; most of
them were missing fingers; some had only bloated, scaly
lumps where their hands should have been.

Yet even the most monstrous of them was watching
Kit hopefully. He could not undo what the pitchblende
had done, as he knew they knew. But perhaps—perhaps—he might yet free them for a cleaner death.

"Keep your eyes open," he said in English. "What I
plan may easily work too well. I can't predict just what
the results will be, but they're certain to be violent."

"Kit—" Paula swallowed and had to stop.

"Can't you be more specific?" Stahl said.

"I could be. But I won't. I don't know whether the
Arab woman speaks English or not, for one thing. All
I can say is, be ready for anything."

"Kit," Paula began again. "I don't doubt that you can
lick that big brute, but there are so many of them—"

"Don't worry," Kit said. "The odds will take care of
themselves in due course. Be sure you take care of yourself, at the first opportunity. Don't stand on ceremony.
Understand?"

"I—I think so."

Kit turned away, wishing he felt half as much con-
fidence as he pretended. True enough, he could probably
best N'mbono, though it would be a contest he would
rather have avoided; but he was counting on the prob-
ability that the black king had not met a well man on
the drum in a long time, perhaps not in over a year.
But what he had to do was a lot more complicated than

simply winning a duel, and it was going to handicap
him severely as a fighter.

N'mbono, oiled and shining in the firelight, stood by
the big drum with arms folded. As Kit approached, he
held out one hand in a ceremonious gesture. In it was
a lamp of stinking pig fat which he had been warming
under his armpit. Kit accepted it gravely and rubbed
a light coat of lard over his chest and arms; Tombu
greased his back.

Billet ladders were brought, thrown up onto the
drumhead, and secured. Either man could have climbed
the drum's lacings handily, but there was only one proper
way of fulfilling this ritual: even death has its polite
formalities. Kit and N'mbono mounted, and the ladders
were cut away.

The two kings faced each other across the taut,
springy hide. The small drums began to thrum softly
in unison.

Kit's bare feet moved on the drum, and under him
the great cask uttered a muffled *whoom*. The sound was
as much felt as heard. N'mbono moved in the opposite
direction, and again the drum sounded.

The skirling water flute struck in. At the same time,
from opposite sides, two heavy black spears came hur-
tling up past the drum head. The two men leaped into
the air after them, hands closing on the spinning
shafts—

Brroooomm!

They struck simultaneously, at the center of the
drum, spear shafts crossed together. For a moment Kit
looked directly into the stone eyes of N'mbono. Then,
with a quick leap, he took his position.

Stamping rhythmically to make unsure his opponent's footing, N'mbono began to stalk him, feinting
with the spear. The stamping was prescribed and very
strict; this was footwork to make that of a European
boxer seem like child's play. Kit stepped and listened,
listened and stepped. He moved rather more quickly
than the warrior, and his steps were lighter. Without
once departing from the configuration of the music below, the great drum took on a rhythm of its own:

Haroom, boom...baroom boom, baroom boom. Haroom, boom...baroom boom, baroom boom.

N'mbono advanced. Kit circled cautiously, listening. The rhythm was not clear enough. It would have to be very clear, with only one note available to him.

With a quick, catlike spring, his opponent leaped forward, the spear stabbing straight for Kit's chest. Kit twisted his body sidewise and parried, jumping away. The drum spoke loudly as he struck the hide, spoiling the sentence, and he tattooed at it with his feet until it roared to blot out any inadvertent word it might have been saying. Then he began to stamp again.

Haroom, boom...baroom boom, baroom boom.

N'mbono was looking a little puzzled. He was not accustomed to the rhythm, and Kit's evolutions did not seem to make much sense to him. (Good; then he was not privy to the language of the *girot*. Not unusual in a king; but a stroke of luck all the same). As Kit continued to retreat, however, he grew more confident, and began to press his advantage. There appeared on his face an expression which Kit had seen often before; it said, plain as day, *Bendele bafa banto*. The music on the ground picked up its tempo excitedly.

Again the black spear darted forward, and again Kit parried. N'mbono slashed back, sweeping the point in viciously, and the stone tip drew a scarlet line across Kit's breast. The slaves groaned, and the warriors shouted exultantly. N'mbono's lips were skinned back from his teeth in a feral grin.

"Does the white stamper taste fear?" he hissed. "Come close, O Ktendi, that my arm may dispatch thee to thy kind little gods."

Haroom, boom...baroom boom, baroom boom.

"My gods are here, and watching," Kit said grimly. He took three long, quick strides which carried him nearly halfway around the rim of the drum. N'mbono pivoted to follow him, and saw what Kit had already seen: the head of Manalendi, poised at about waist height, swaying gently with the hypnotic rhythms but following their every movement.

N'mbono swallowed, and said: "Ktendi fears. He retreats, and calls *juju* to his aid. This is not well done."

A worthy opponent; that taunt must have come hard.

"Manalendi will not interfere," Kit said. But this might well be untrue; Kit had no way of knowing.

For answer, the warrior flexed his knees and made the stretched hide give sharply. Kit lost his balance and went down on one knee. In the same sinuous motion N'mbono launched himself forward on the upward reflex of the drumhead.

It was too fast an attack for Kit to bring his own spear into play. He had no choice but to close his hand hard around the other's spearhead. He could feel the tendons in his palm parting; a terrific stab of pain shot up his forearm. But it diverted the stroke from his exposed side.

His free arm locked around the other's thighs, and he stood up with a back-wrenching heave, his shoulder digging into N'mbono's stomach. The warrior grunted and fell back, but not before Kit had snatched up his own spear again and inflicted a heavy cut across one hip.

The drum rolled like angry thunder to the struggle, and the shouts and cries from below redoubled. Kit stomped again, picking up the old rhythm, and circled warily. He had to use his left hand now for the spear, for the other one was useless; he could no longer close it. The shaft was slippery with blood from his unthinking attempt to shift back to the right hand after the hip thrust. It was the worst luck possible; he would have to try and finish this long before he had intended to, or be defeated by sheer loss of blood.

Haroom, boom ... baroom boom, baroom boom.

N'mbono was playing it close now, poised for the kill. His spear arm darted at Kit like an adder.

"The mighty Ktendi is fallen," he gloated. "There is much wailing in the Gundu lands, for Ktendi has met a brave man."

"Not brave enough," Kit panted. The pace was getting too fast for him to control it. If only he could keep up the rhythm for a few seconds more....

But N'mbono had other plans. He had at last realized that Kit had some reason for preferring the present beat, and deliberately set out to distract him from it.

He sprang up and down on the drumhead. The great instrument rang to every impact. Kit's following beats were lost in the uproar; he was having trouble keeping his footing.

"Time's up," he thought regretfully.

Without a moment's hesitation he charged across the drum at the tribesman, his head down like a battering ram. N'mbono's jaw dropped. In the second it took him to bring his guard up, Kit was upon him. The heavy sticks clattered and crashed; sparks flew as the points slid off each other.

N'mbono's great arms locked about Kit's waist, pinning his shaft against his chest. Kit kicked him hard in the shins—not much of a blow in bare feet, but enough to enable him to break free, throwing the other backward against the drumhead. The impact made him stagger, but somehow he stayed on his feet.

The enemy chief came back like a rubber ball. He hurled himself forward with all the fury of a charging water buffalo, his spear point cleaving the steaming air before him.

Kit drew back his left arm and threw. His spear whistled, and drove in just under the point of N'mbono's jaw. The warrior's throat was fountaining bright blood even before he struck the reverberating skins. Kit wrenched himself sidewise sharply, but the falling body struck his shoulder and he went down with it.

N'mbono was dead when Kit struggled out from under him, good hand clapped over the rent in his side that the dead man's spear had made. He walked to the center of the drum and stamped ceremoniously.

Haroom, boom...baroom boom, baroom boom. Haroom, boom...baroom boom, baroom boom.

The last thunder of the drum died, and the distant mountain threw back the echoes.

Kit walked wearily to the rim of the drum and waited until a ladder was thrown up to him; then he perforce let go of his side wound to tie the top of the billet fast. Down below, the tribesmen stood in a silent ring.

As he touched the ground, one of them ran agilely up the ladder and scooped up N'mbono's spear. With a

single broad jump which made the drum shout trium-
phantly, he vaulted to the ground and held the spear
out to Kit.

"The nation of Ktendi welcomes its lord," he cried
in singsong.

Solemnly Kit took the spear. A great, composite
"Haiie!" went up from the warriors, and the wild rat-
tling and pounding and skirling went up all over again.

Kit leaned the new spear against his chest and handed
his own to Tombu.

"You'd better put a couple of corks in me here and
there," he said in French. "Was it long enough, do you
think?"

"I cannot know, *bwana,*" Tombu murmured. He
picked up one of Kit's discarded puttees and began to
bind his slashed hand with it. "We will hope so. I knew
what you were saying, but without the tune, it might
have been almost anything. Who can say?"

"None," Kit agreed reluctantly. He took over the
bandaging job, pulling it tight with his teeth, while
Tombu stripped a plantain leaf and plastered it against
his side. Then he stepped forward toward the throne of
Nanan.

The Asiatic girl was watching him with an enigmatic
smile.

"Well fought, Ktendi," she said. "Are you prepared
to serve the Rock God as well as you serve the death
drum?"

This proposition was not unexpected; Kit had an answer ready for it. But he was not allowed to give it.

"No, he isn't," van Bleyswijck's voice growled.

The Belgian marine was striding toward them. He
had a carbine on his arm, a Newton-designed Savage
.22 which had not been in evidence among his baggage
on the trek. It was primarily for maribou, monkeys,
and other small game, but at this range it could kill a
man very nicely; and it was pointing straight at Kit.

"Hello, van Bleyswijck," Kit said quietly.

"Don't hello me, you white nigger," the marine
snarled. "I told Stahl we'd be fools to hire you." He
swung on Nanan. "And I told you we'd be fools to play
along with this, too. Now look what's happened."

The woman did not stop smiling.

"All things have an end," she said, with unctuous piety. "You had begun to weary me, Piet. And it was stupid of you to kill the doctor—we needed him. Be grateful for a worthy successor. That is the best compliment a woman can give at such a time."

"Dead men," van Bleyswijck said, "succeed nobody." He raised the carbine.

"You're a fool," Kit said sharply. "You might get out of here alive, if you leave now. Don't you know that this tribe has just taken me as their chief?"

"They've been taking orders from me for a long time," the marine said. "They'll do it again if it comes to that."

"Oh? And then what will you do? You'll have to pass through Wassabi country again to stay in business. I am king of the Wassabi too, and they know I'm here. What will you tell them when you come out without me? I'd like to hear it; it had better be good."

"*Lokuta te,*" Tombu said, grinning wolfishly. Of course it *was* in fact a lie; but under the circumstances it was true for van Bleyswijck, which was what Tombu was grinning about.

After a moment, the marine lowered the gun a little.

"All right," he said. "I'm in no hurry. I think I'll just wait until you make the first move, Kennedy. What will it be? Will you order your nation to give up their Rock God, and throw all the pitchblende in the river? Or try to free their slaves? That would be interesting. Why don't you try it?"

"Whatever I do, you'll probably get killed in the process—unless you turn yourself over to Stahl at once," Kit said, shrugging. "If you're a prisoner of Belgium, you may have some slight chance of surviving."

Van Bleyswijck laughed and walked away. Nanan watched him go with narrowed eyes. Finally she said:

"Piet is a fool, as you say. He does not know that you are of us and of the jungle, not of his European world. He thinks you were only showing off, up there on the drum."

Kit struck his spear of kingship into the ground by the butt.

"You also are a fool, Nanan," he said stonily. "What

do you know of the jungle? You grew up in a whorehouse in Tangiers, if I'm any judge. Do you think the folk of the jungle do *this* to each other—he gestured at the raddled slaves—"without the prompting of 'civilized' people? Van Bleyswijck is right. I mean to stop this slaving for pitchblende. There is no place in the jungle for that kind of foulness."

The woman sprang up, her eyes blazing. "Close your mouth! Do you think your petty killing gives you any rights to *me?* One word from me, and you are only another lump of dung. *Mnote!*"

A tribesman leaped forward and touched his forehead to the ground, pouring dust over the back of his head.

"Return the white prisoners to their hut," Nanan said in Swahili. "And drive the slaves to their sties."

"Stop," Kit said.

The African halted in mid-step and turned back toward Kit. It was plain that the unfortunate warrior did not find the ground between the frying pan and the fire comfortable. Kit dismissed him with a brusque gesture, and stood fast until the man backed away into the darkness. Then he mounted the mound of earth on which the throne stood. He faced the restive tribe.

"Ktendi," he boomed, "declares the Rock God a false god and a night shape. He declares the traffic with the mountain at an end. He declares the slaves free to return to the lands of their fathers." He raked the amazed faces with unblinking eyes. "He declares the white woman Nanan to be a leech, and will have her cast from the gates of the boma. He declares that the white prisoners are freed. *Kosala pila moko ngai koloba.*"

A low muttering went through the crowd, swelling rapidly. Van Bleyswijck stood to one side in the firelight smiling mockingly, cradling the carbine. Without pause, Kit reached out with his good hand, grasped Nanan by the hair at her scruff, and propelled her off the mound ahead of him. She screeched like escaping steam until he cuffed her with the back of his bad hand, opening his wound and clashing blood down her neck and the front of her abaiyia, then she choked and stopped.

Tombu appeared silently out of nowhere and walked

beside them. The ranks did not part. The first motion
made toward getting out of Kit's way was met by an
equally determined one to stand fast. Nanan struck
backward at him suddenly, but her reach was short.
Kit twisted his hand in her greasy hair and marched
her steadily down the path toward the gate.

Then she found her voice again. "Kill!" she screamed
breathlessly, writhing under his hand. "Kill the white
man! *Ayang*.... OW! You pig-dog—"

The massed ranks wavered and shrank back: Ktendi
was a man to be feared, that was certain; *je makasi*, a
man strong and of mighty heart, and master of much
juju—the very serpents listened to his voice; and a great
dancer before Father Death. Yet the woman Nanan was
also very strong; strong with the blasting strength of
the Rock God—

"Ktendi has spoken," Tombu said. With the point of
Kit's spear, he drew a little arc deep just between his
eyebrows. The blood began to ooze down his nose. "Make
way."

There was another hiss of breath from the darkness,
and the path cleared a little. Then there was a cry, and
a small, fiercely painted warrior, the one Nanan had
called Mnote—sprang directly before them.

"Ktendi hath spoken evil!" he shouted, in the cracked
voice of a hysteric. "He is a sorcerer! He hath slain
N'mbono not by courage, but by dark arts!"

Whatever the little warrior's intentions might have
been, this did not turn out to be a reassuring tack. An
immense hand grasped him by the biceps and yanked
him back. Instantly there was a whirlpool of violence
in the darkness, and the hand's owner was writhing
and screaming in the dust, a spearhead driven into his
kidneys. The spearman came howling out of the ranks
at Kit, barehanded.

Kit hurled Nanan straight into the man's out-
stretched arms.

"Slaves!" he shouted at the top of his voice. "Ktendi
speaks! You are slaves no more! Arise, attack, seek out
your lodges! *Ayang!*"

The clarion summons made the very jungle ring. The

milling, radium-eaten slaves called it back hoarsely,
eagerly, ready now to believe anything.

"Ayang!"

The warriors of Kit's brief kingdom were already at
each other's throats, split into two groups by conflicting
loyalties. As was only to have been expected, those
clinging to the older allegiance seemed to be in the large
majority. Van Bleyswijck had vanished.

"Quick, Tombu—get Stahl and the woman over here."
Kit slammed the flat of the spear blade against a charging warrior's temple and retreated, his point making a
flashing half-circle of death before him. Tombu cut his
way toward the spot where the whites had been held,
and was met halfway—Stahl had already grabbed a
fallen bush knife and was doing plenty of damage. Kit
backed toward them.

"Paula," he panted. "Knife in my boot—my right
hand's no good—"

The girl bent and snatched the knife out. With it,
she no longer seemed half so naked; a change had come
over her; she looked frighteningly fierce.

"Now what?" Stahl demanded. "This is a fine civil
war you have here, Kennedy!"

"First class," Kit agreed. "Head for the river gate,
quick. It's our only chance."

As if in answer, a hoarse, screaming hiss sounded
from the direction of the river: *"Hhhouchgh!*

"God in Heaven!" Stahl said. "What's that?"

"Trouble, aren't you used to it yet? Run, all of you!"

They ran. Kit and Tombu fought rear-guard. The
earsplitting, coughing hiss sounded again. Around them
the warriors, by common, unspoken assent, had given
over fighting with each other and were running, seemingly in all directions, but with obvious purposiveness
all the same.

"Hurry!" Kit panted. "If we don't make that gate in
time—"

The river gate finally came in sight. Along the high
wall a myriad torches were traveling, and past the re-
treating party scores of spearmen ran for vine ladders.
Again the awful sound rent the air.

"Kit!" Paula gasped. "What *is* that noise?"

"Mokele-mbemba."

"What!"

"Yes. Hurry, or we'll be cut off. The drumming and the excitement must have made him angry."

The wall rocked to a heavy blow.

"Too late," he said. "Stahl! Stop running, we've got to fight our way back. Maybe they'll be too busy to waste much time on us."

The wall shook again. The blow seemed to come from rather high off the ground outside: the logs were splintering and cracking nearly five feet above the top of the gate. The torches sailed off the wall in long trails of sparks and disappeared, falling toward the river like malign comets. More were passed up along the ladders.

"No good," Kit said. "That beast hasn't sense enough to be very afraid of fire, I'll wager. I'm afraid we're goners, my friends."

"Why?" Stahl demanded, flourishing his knife. "If we can't—"

Half a dozen tree trunks in the wall burst like a salvo of cannon. In the breach, a gray, circular foot, like the pad of an impossibly huge elephant, protruded for a moment, then struggled and was yanked back. Again the wall shook, and tribesmen fell off it like apples from a shaken tree. High above came the futile spitting of a carbine; but it was not maribou, monkeys, men and other small game that van Bleyswijck was shooting at now.

Kit's party struggled back through the stream of panicking, screaming tribesmen, but it was like swimming in a swamp: every inch won seemed to use up an hour. The universe seemed filled with wide-stretched, howling mouths, filed teeth and jutting needle-pointed ivory nose-ornaments. Kit kept the knife out of play as much as possible. Though he and the rest of the party were taking a battering from the shields of the warriors, the running men seemed otherwise oblivious of them.

For the last time, the high wall groaned and swayed. Then, with a despairing howl of tortured wood and a volley of parting vines, a whole section collapsed.

Mokele-mbemba stood in the breach.

For a long moment there was dead silence, except

for the thin wailing of the injured. *Mokele-mbemba's*
head, not wholly unlike that of an enormous rhinoceros,
turned back and forth in the firelight, the small eyes
blinking with stupid viciousness. He had not one horn,
but three—long curved scimitars, one at the nose, the
other two sprouting like those of an antelope from the
forehead. The back of his skull flared out into a bony
shield which completely covered his shoulders; the great
carapace jostled the broken trunks as he looked this
way and that. And beyond the shield was a barrellike
body, propped up on squat legs, also like those of a
rhino; along his spine there stood a double row of dia-
mond-shaped bony plates, about the size of a man's
hand near the head, but growing larger to the center
of the arched back. An African woman cowered right
beside him, cradling a child, only partly shielded by the
sagging poles of the wall, but *mokele-mbemba* could not
see her; she was in the blind spot of his great shoulder-
shield.

"Herrgott!" Stahl breathed. "A—a stegosaur! *Es ist
ganz unmöglich!"*

The great beast lowered his head and screamed again,
without opening its parrot's beak more than slightly.
It began to lumber forward.

The ground shook.

And then, like a bolt of living lightning, Manalendi
hurdled his long spotted body forward. The python was
upon the river beast almost before Kit saw it—coil after
coil, lashing about the creature's chest and legs, flowing, constricting....

The monster jerked its head up and back, the great
jaws parting to pluck at the living cable around one
front leg; but its carapace did not allow its head much
play. Manalendi flowed out of range, and struck back.
He struck at the base of the neck, and his head caromed
off the bone collar like a skipping stone. The second
time he was luckier; his fangs sank deep into the tough
hide of the throat, where the bone did not extend.

The river beast tried to swing around, but for a moment its heavy tail was arrested by the rocking timbers.
Then the tail came free. Kit was stunned to see that it

bore at its end another cluster of horns, no less than six of them, like a giant spur.

It screamed again. Manalendi tightened his grip and the scream choked off.

Blindly, the monster charged the wall. It missed the opening it had made; the impact seemed to shake the world.

Kit herded his charges away from the epochal struggle.

"Sorry," he said through clenched teeth. "But the big one will trample most of this area before he's beaten. We'll have to use every minute."

"I want to stay," Stahl said, pulling back. "That monster—there has never been such an opportunity—dissect the body, make drawings—it will stun every scientist in the world—"

"Your assignment," Kit told him, "is finished. March!"

For a long time after dawn, Kit and Tombu drove the exhausted Paula and Stahl mercilessly across the sterile grassy plateau and on through the silent forest of doum-palms. It was not until they reached the bottom of the rise leading to the grassland that Kit allowed a halt. By that time he was carrying Paula, who had fainted, and Tombu had Stahl's arm over his shoulder. Kit wondered if Stahl remembered having struck the *capita*, only a mile or so from here. Tombu had doubtless forgotten it completely.

"Awa," Kit said. *"Oyo esika biso tolalaki."*

The Bantu let go of Stahl, who sat down heavily. Kit expected him to keel over at once, but the Belgian's curiosity was insatiable.

"Why so far?" he demanded at once.

"Protection," Kit said, grinning wearily. "I didn't dance on the drum just to wake the big river beast. I knew that no matter what happened, some of Nanan's tribe would be likely to follow us. I had to call the Wassabi."

"Call the—? You mean you fought that African chief just to send a message?"

"No, not just to send a message, Herr Stahl. But that was part of it. There wasn't any other drum in that *kraal* big enough to be heard as far as Lake Wassabi, and I knew we'd need a *poshi* long before we hit Gundu country. We'd have had one on the way in, too, if it hadn't been for those damned marines."

The brush rustled, and Tombu raised his hand in the three signs of peace. Tall, broad-shouldered tribesmen melted into the little clearing, saluted Kit and Tombu as one salutes kings, and spoke softly to the Bantu. Tombu drew diagrams on the earth with the butt of his spear. Stahl said:

"You're an incredible person. No wonder they make legends of your doings. I believe you must really be a king."

"I am a king twice over; and I assure you that it *is* better to reign in Hell than serve in Heaven."

Stahl blinked. He seemed to recognize the text. Finally he said:

"Nein wohl. But I still have another question. How on earth did you know that van Bleyswijck, of all people, was the pitchblende runner?"

"That," Kit said, "was guesswork, with a leaven of logic. If Belgium was to launch an investigation of the business, where was there a safer place for the headman than in the middle of the investigators? As soon as I found out that you were clean, I had only one other suspect—the Lees were English, after all. The only thing that really puzzled me was what was in it for van Bleyswijck."

"Money," Stahl said. "That's usually sufficient."

"No. Not in Africa, Herr Stahl. I have more money than I know how to count; you probably know that I live over a gold mine, quite literally. But in this country there is nothing to spend it on, if you have to live here— as a member of the colonial marines obviously must. And he was a young man, with no family abroad to drive him into cupidity. There had to be something else. When I saw the woman, I had the answer."

"The world is full of women," Stahl said dubiously.

"Yes, too full. But I doubt that van Bleyswijck had ever encountered one like Nanan before. Arab women are schooled in love; it is the only science that they are absolutely required to know. I have seen men go to perdition on that account before—Europeans, of course, always. And the sad thing is, they always get the carrion, and aren't even aware of it; no Arab gentleman would look twice at such a piece of used meat as Nanan; but to a European, it's a new world. Pfah."

"Mr. Kennedy, I wouldn't have believed it possible, but I think you embarrass me. Nevertheless, go on."

Kit grinned again. "That's almost the end of the story—though I may have to rub your nose in your prejudices once more, at that. Women like Nanan know what they are, even when their European lovers don't. They know only the one way to climb higher in the European world—their own world is shut to them— and that is by acquiring a new and more powerful man. I set out to be that man, to put van Bleyswijck on the outside and make him lay his cards down where you could see them. After that, it was just a matter of stirring up enough conflict to divert attention from us."

"And you warned me," Stahl said ruefully, "that you might succeed a little too well. I am beyond surprise now. I believe *mokele-mbemba* has made me immune, from now on."

Kit thought a long time. At last he said:

"There is no end to surprises in this country, I'm afraid. To begin with, that creature was not *mokele-mbemba*."

"Not—?"

"No. Probably it's related to *mokele-mbemba*. It lives in the same kind of place, and it seems to eat the same food. Sad, in a way; did you see the beast's mouth when it screamed? It's a plant eater—not dangerous at all except for its size and stupidity. But it doesn't answer to the description of *mokele-mbemba* at all. Wherever that night shape lives, we have yet to flush it out."

"The thing we saw was a *Triceratops*," Stahl said, beginning to become excited despite his utter weariness. "And where there is one there must be others; cows, to carry on the line; at least one herd, somewhere! And if *mokele-mbemba* is a different species—listen, Kit, we must find out these things! We dare not let it slip from our hands! If you would be so kind as to take me on again, after we reach the coast, we could organize

a safari, organize it properly to run down this legend
for good and all—"

Paula stirred in her bed of rushes. "Kit," she moaned.
"Kit."

Kit nodded politely to Stahl and stood up.

"That's not for me," he said. "I will not go hunting
the night shapes, whatever they are. I know better.
...Excuse me."

He went in quietly and lay down beside her, touching
her forehead with the tip of his nose as the shaman had
taught him. Her fever had subsided a little, which was
good; but she was wakeful.

"Kit. Oh, don't go away."

"I'm not going. Rest. You're still pretty hot."

She turned toward him, groping. "I'm cold, I'm cold.
And you are going. I took it all and you've gone already.
All those animals! Oh, God, all those animals!"

He unlocked her arms as gently as he could, but
abruptly he found that he could not be very gentle.
"Stop that. You're sick, Paula. If you won't rest, I'll
have to have the boys bathe you again, and give you a
drug. Better to quit now and sleep naturally, so we can
get you to the coast and a doctor."

"I had a doctor," she whispered raggedly. "He never
did me any good. And he let that bloody little Belgian
toy soldier kill him!"

She sobbed quietly and was silent again.

"Paula?"

"Go away."

"All right; have a good sleep. We'll have to leave
early."

There was no answer. Evidently reason had pre-
vailed...yet he had an annoying, an infuriating conviction that it hadn't. He sat up resignedly, favoring
the ache in his groin; he had so many aches already
that he hardly noticed it. Outside, some of the boys were
humming somnolently beside the last of the fire, a water
song, a nasal and scriptural, without beginning or end,
final and Hamitic, water without world, night without
end, day without source.

"Kit...."

"Yes, Paula."

"Kit.... don't let me die."

"I won't. But you have to sleep."

"I.... No. No. Don't let me sleep. Kit, it isn't fair. It isn't fair. Kit, I can't. I can't sleep. I can't go to sleep, not like that. Don't let me. Please, don't let me."

"Paula—you need to mend. And for that we need speed. I promise you—"

"Don't promise me," she said raggedly. "Touch me. I don't want your damn promises. I want somebody to make me back into a woman again. After that, the hell with you, Kit Kennedy, you white nigger, but *in the name of God will you kindly touch me?*"

Outside, the song stopped; and, defeated, Kit lay back in the thick darkness.

V *The Lodge*

Kit stepped out of his lodge onto the springy turf and took a deep breath. All around him the baobab trees towered, except directly back of the lodge, where the mountain began. Pearly morning light filtered through the leaves onto the deep, rich green of the loam. Over the sonorous whispering of the nearby river, there came a chittering of monkeys, and the sound of a scampering game being played invisibly high up among the leaves.

Kit sighed. Here, in the deep Gunda province, it was cool and clear most of the day in this season. The coast was the steaming country, where white men wasted and died quickly, yellow with the jaundice of alcohol, their ears ringing with quinine. Here he was not even a white man, and he had no encumbrances. He should be satisfied. He *was* satisfied. What was the matter, anyhow?

The wind shifted slightly and Kit felt a delicate pulsing in his ears, as if tiny paws were pattering directly on his eardrums. He stiffened and turned. Yes, sure enough; there was a word in the air, from a long way away, somewhere down by the Luberfu. After a while the thrumming became stronger, as the Wassabi village *girot* picked up the message and passed it along.

Over Kit's head the foliage stirred, and a great, flat wedge dipped down to stare at the lone man. Kit grinned wrily.

"Hello, Manalendi. Hear something?"

The python shot out its forked tongue and withdrew it with the quickness of lightning. To that tongue the noise was painfully loud, and probably obscured sounds in which the snake was really interested, sounds no human being could hear. The huge head wove uneasily.

Kit could be of no help. Manalendi's overwhelming curiosity never failed to amuse him, but fundamentally he still did not like having been adopted by a twenty-five-foot constrictor. The creature had been following him around for nearly a year now, sleeping somewhere near the lodge, departing only on brief trips to snitch a chicken or a pig from the Wassabi; and who could say what that meant?

Kit resisted the temptation to believe that he understood it, even partially. It was true that he had something of an affinity for snakes, ever since that memorable summer at a boy's camp when a beautiful king snake had adopted the cabin in which the eight-year-old Kit slept, and had allowed him alone to handle the living cable—even to carry it about, coiled drily around one arm, tail high, head at wrist. He had rapidly lost all fear of snakes as a class, and soon thereafter had learned to respect them; but to understand them? That was something else again.

In the past year he had allowed no one to molest Manalendi, not even the justifiably resentful tribesmen on whom he was poaching; and once, with unusual foolhardiness, he had helped the awesome mass of power through one session of its only recurrent crisis—the shedding of its skin. That had been downright crazy, for Manalendi had been very bad-tempered about it! Only the fact that he was also torpid had gotten Kit through it alive. Yet always thereafter he had seemed more amenable to being touched, to the point where he now allowed himself to be searched for mites—one affliction even he in his power could do nothing about for himself—though only for a yard or so at a time. Kit did not particularly care for this new custom, either, but he kept it up out of honest doubts as to the safety of discontinuing it.

Above all, it would be mortally easy to fall into the error of thinking that one of the two—man or snake—had become the pet of the other. Death would be hot on the heels of any such assumption.

In fact, there was no safe assumption. Nobody could *know* why Manalendi did not go home. Were it possible to ask him, he too might well have no answer; or it might be that the question itself might be fatal. There are some facts one simply has to abide, especially if one of them is twenty-five feet long and will not go away.

The drum message was still a little garbled, but there was no doubt that it said something about white men. That was always bad news in this country and perhaps Manalendi knew it. He plainly hated drum noise, yet it always brought him out; it was Kit's guess that the python equated drums with trouble—if he were lucky, interesting trouble which would wind up in a fight. Manalendi was cold, but not vicious, and most of the jungle creatures big enough to match him left him strictly alone; it was, Kit supposed, a dull life for the most part.

But the python was a hole card which Kit had hopes of playing again. If possible, it ought not to be betrayed ahead of time. He gave the snake the one-word command he thought he had been able to teach it.

"Upstairs, handsome."

Manalendi refused to understand. After a moment, Kit spoke again, and rapped the cruel nose sharply with his closed fist. The snake drew back into an enormous, menacing S, taut in midair.

"Upstairs, handsome."

Manalendi shot out his tongue. Then, slowly, he withdrew, his dappled blue body blending with the shifting leaves. Kit resumed breathing. He had lived through another interview; but they were all different, providing no pattern or guidance for the next; the ham-

mer at the end of that S might just as well have brained
him.

The drumming went on. Kit looked speculatively at
his own drums, which hung, their drawstrings flaccid,
from the eaves of his lodge. Then he decided against it.
He was a stammering drummer at best, and were the
matter urgent enough to arouse Tombu, he'd already
be on the way, since the Wassabi tribes were the ones
now passing the message.

The thought had barely entered his head when he
saw the brawny shape of the African king sprinting
silently down the trail toward the lodge. Kit made the
three signs.

"Long life, Tombu."

"A thousand years," Tombu said automatically. Then:
"Ktendi! There is a safari coming here, a great one,
with many guns, and many boys. They have whips."

"Whips? Real ones? Not the *sjambok?*"

"No, *bondele,* long plaited whips such as white men
use on slaves. Already they have had many desertions.
The deserters claim such cruelty as might frighten a
Belgian."

A joke; then the matter was serious. Kit said, "What's
it all about? Why do the boys have to be driven? Doesn't
the *baas* pay enough?"

"The pay is high," Tombu said, squatting down on
the turf with the natural grace of a creature to which
furniture could be nothing but a crutch. Kit followed.
"But there are whispers."

"There are always whispers. These people probably
hope for gold. Maybe they want to get it from me—
most of the whites know how I pay for my shells. There's
a silly story about a hidden ancient temple under my
hut—you've heard it. White men will believe anything."

"No, *bondele.* One can sense the gold fever; it shows
in the eyes, and in the smell of the sweat. Besides, who
would disturb Ktendi's gold? This is something else.
They are said to be seeking the shapes."

"No."

"I tell you so."

Kit's lips whitened. "If it were not for the bearers,"

he said grimly, "one might almost wish that they find the shapes. This is very bad, Tombu. How came they to hear of the shapes? Do the deserters know?"

"Yes, they know. They are hard to talk to, but they know. We are to blame, Ktendi. They have heard of the shape that we saw. They have collected stories from warriors and chiefs; now they are talking to shamans; they believe in the shapes now and want to hunt them, such fools they are."

"*Lokuta te*. We are to blame. They will have to be stopped."

All in all, Kit was not surprised, though he was thoroughly disgusted. What footling admiration for Stahl's courage had prevented him from killing the fat little man when it had been practicable? Letting him get back to Europe with a tale of having seen a living *Triceratops* obviously was asking for trouble. Yet Kit had let him go, for no better fee than a promise not to come back.

And now here he was again, or someone probably much like him.

There was an abundance of evidence to lead them on, once they had accepted the bare possibility that such an animal might still survive in Africa. The shapes were a matter of common experience—not counting, for the moment, those which were not "real" in any sense a European could admit. The tribesmen, who knew no geology, accepted them with only a shudder; to them *mokele-mbemba*, the snake-headed *lau*, the Elephant-Eater, and all the others were frightful, but after all fundamentally only a few of the million heads of Father Death. *Ibwa wete joi ja nkakamwa;* that covered the matter.

To the European world, however, which knew these creatures only as faint traces in ancient rocks, such a discovery could not possibly be anything less than an explosion, no matter how conservatively, even incredulously, it was greeted at first. Long ago, Kit had known a white naturalist so fanatic on the subject that he cherished a thing called coprolith—a fossilized dinosaur dropping. He had used it for a paperweight.

But Kit had let Stahl go, and hardly a month had passed before he had become aware that Stahl, back in

Belgium, was babbling. The first hint of it had turned up in one of Paula's letters from home; it had precipitated one of their many scarifying quarrels.

For these Kit blamed nobody but himself. He had been a damned fool to let her stay at all, knowing as well as he did how much she had to learn, and how little time he would be able to devote to teaching her. It speedily developed that his long years of isolation had left him with much to learn, too.

Kit had made no offer of marriage, nor had Paula ever raised the question. After a while, however, Kit had thought it incumbent on him to offer the explanation she had not asked for. As an explanation, it was a model of logic, to which no reasonable person could have objected: Paula was still a subject of the Crown and had some residual status back home—damaged though it must have been by her association with him, this was not a liaison susceptible to anything a court might call proof—as the widow of another servant of Her Majesty. On the other hand, were she to marry a stateless person, and under the aegis of Belgium at that, her legal immunities and recourses would probably be lost.

Paula had granted all this in one second and dismissed it in the next. She did not care about the logic, but instead tunneled directly through it to the buried assumption on which it rested—the assumption that she would someday go back to England, rather than staying with Kit forever.

That quarrel had been the first—and only the first of many, fundamentally, because it had never been resolved. The occasional letters from London exacerbated it each and every time. They came from Paula's one remaining loyal friend, a woman in the Whitehall circle who seemed to imagine Paula's life to be romantic, and Kit to be a noble savage out of Rousseau. What seemed to Kit to be an offhand and certainly mild comment on the woman's monumental silliness had sparked another explosion. Eventually, he had taken to postponing essential trips to the coast, and, when he finally did go, avoiding LeClerc, so as not to have to ask for or be forced to accept any mail; which, of course, Paula detected effortlessly.

Worst of all, she was often sick; she had none of the essential immunities. Those days and weeks were the most desperate of all....

Well, she was gone now, leaving behind a cold exhaustion of all feeling which Kit had no trouble recognizing. He had carried it with him ever since Kansas. It was his armor, such as it was, against self-reproach. He wore under it the bitterness, the alum-and-lye corrosion of his hatred for the whole white world.

Yet how could he blame Paula? Her background had overridden her, too. She had yearned for it inevitably after they had fought; yearned for the sound of nasal voices politely discussing things of no moment, yearned to be back where the food was cooked and the nearest snake—Manalendi had increasingly given her the horrors—could be assumed to be at least fifty miles away, and only a few inches long, to boot. In the end she had demanded a *poshi* of Tombu, and had left Kit's lodge for the—for her—long trek to Berghe Ste. Marie and civilization. With her she had taken Kit's last twinge of sympathy for the white man's world...plus certain other intangibles he did not think about anymore.

Nevertheless: Paula had been some kind of investigator—hardly a nabob, he supposed, but at the very least an authorized agent—for the Congo Inquiry Commission. If she had confirmed any part of Stahl's story of seeing an ancient monster in a Congolese swamp, the Admiralty would say, "My dear girl!"—but they'd believe her.

However it had happened, it had happened. Now there was a safari looking for that valley, and for the shapes...looking in the old familiar European way: with whips.

Tombu was watching Kit steadily.

"How would you?" he said. "An advance party to blunt the edges of these seekers? A war arrow would speed desertions, and we might let the whites go on without boys until they flounder. After that..." The big Bantu did not bother to finish the sentence; in another sense, it had already been passed.

Kit shook his head.

"This safari is probably official," he said. "If we break it up, we'll give the whites every excuse they'd need for a punitive foray—soldiers, whippings, hands cut off, burning of villages, dynamite ... all just as before. The English have subdued the Leopold devil, a little—do we want it back?"

"But if they find the valley, Ktendi, the same thing will happen. The *bondele* will pour in by tens and tens and tens, to shoot at the shapes. Or worse."

"True," Kit said, rising. "At best, they will turn the Gundu country into a reservation overnight. Or they might find a herd of the shapes, and scatter it—"

"Do you think there are herds?"

"Who knows? Do you think there are not?"

Tombu bent his head slightly; he knew a forensic point when he heard one; he was not a king for nothing.

"If there is such a nest in the valley," he said, "and the shapes are turned out of it, no man would set foot in the whole of Katanga again, no, not even his grand-childrens' grandchildren. I ask you again, Ktendi, what would you? If we may not stop this safari by war, with what are we left?"

"It may come to war in the end," Kit said soberly. "But we can't dare it yet. First, I think, I want to see Atumbi. I'll need you with me."

The African stared at Kit for a long moment. Kit could hardly fault him for his doubt. Atumbi was the wizard of the Wassabi; there was no love lost between him and Tombu, for here as among all the Congo peoples king and witch doctor were constant rivals for the ultimate power.

"Atumbi hates you, Ktendi," the king said at last. "And *juju* is a weak reed against whips and guns."

"My brother, whips and guns impress you overmuch; when did you and I last need either? As for *juju*, I've no use for Atumbi's kind. But look you, Tombu: you told me yourself that these whites are beginning to talk to shamans—as is only sensible, since it's the shapes they're hunting, and the shapes are of the devil king-dom. Hence what I want first from Atumbi is silence—and for that, I must have his king behind me."

"Lokuta te," Tombu said, showing all his teeth.

"Then quickly. We have little time."

Tombu surged to his feet without further question and went sprinting down the trail, Kit at his heels.

Behind Kit there was a sudden rustle of leaves and fronds: the sound of Manalendi alarmed. But when Kit cast over his shoulder to see what was the matter, the python was not in sight. There was nothing but a diminishing fall of dead vine leaves and detached orchid petals, sifting down to the turf before the lodge like a thin drizzle of broken oaths. The sound whispered away over his head. It might have been going north, but Kit could not be sure; the silence returned too quickly.

He looked up, but of course saw nothing. Manalendi was gone—but where and why could not be riddled. He might be back to the lodge before sunset. It might be that what had alarmed him was of no significance at all to men, no matter what their color.

Or it might be that he had at last started back to his home valley, where he had, a year ago, killed an ancient of his reptile tribe...and where, perhaps, others still churned the swamps of Paradise, plucked the white translucent fruits from the lianas, fought and mated titanically, or chewed their weeds over dim memories of things that had happened before there was such a creature as man.

With a scalp-prickling chill, Kit turned his face ahead, and discovered that Tombu too had disappeared around a sharp turn of the green-blue tunnel of the trail. Ducking his head and hunching his shoulders, Kit ran faster, listening to the thudding music of the drums.

In the hut of Atumbi there was a peculiar, ineradicable stench, compounded of smoke, blood, scorched flesh, orts, and a variety of aromatic herbs—the reek of the fetish. The hut was also very dark, but that was usual. The darkness was chinked with sunlight, sufficient to reveal the fat ugliness of Atumbi—fat with the kind of power which is never challenged to a trial of strength, ugly with fears and hatreds the truly strong never need to feel.

Kit made a slight, ceremonial bow and grinned tightly

into the murk. He had no more than the usual number of enemies, but he was glad to number witch doctors among them. That *juju* existed was a matter he did not doubt, but in his experience few of the tribal devil dancers knew more about it than the rest of the tribesmen. They were simply parasites, preying upon the universal African belief that no man ever dies a natural death, but instead only of some application of malice and magic, brought about by a curse.

Kit had had deadly curses placed upon him by more of these leeches than he could remember, and had survived them without any more effort than might have been put into a shrug. It was simply a matter of keeping magic and power separate from each other—and bearing in mind that both were real, in their several universes. Not every shaman was a charlatan: there was an old man to the southwest, for example, who might make a bad enemy....

The tubby sorcerer apparently did not like Kit's grin. He bent a black look upon Tombu.

"Thine omens are evil, great chief," he said sonorously. He had a surprisingly deep voice, only a little spoiled by an asthmatic wheeze at the end of each speech. "This day have I read thy fate in the entrails of a pure-white rooster. Thou bringest thy people toward dire ends, through overmuch hearkening to strangers and devils."

"There are no messages writ in such messes," Tombu said, using the infinitely insulting *dju,* a grammatical construction ordinarily reserved for animals and children. "Thy chicken bespeaks thine own jealousy and nothing more. Ktendi is no stranger to any but thyself. Leave off thy prattling, Atumbi—there's kings' work afoot."

Atumbi grumbled and wheezed, but no words came through. Tombu was still his chief, whatever he might think about Kit. At last he said:

"You speak of the safari, that is easily read. Of this Atumbi was warned, long ago and long."

Kit stepped forward; it seemed to him that this duel had gone on long enough. Now that the tribal courtesies

and insults had been rehearsed and satisfied, he might
enter the ritual without an overt breach of custom.

"Then perhaps Atumbi can advise Ktendi," he said,
"who must learn what little he knows from the drums.
Did the spirits have to report to Atumbi that the safari
is here to hunt night shapes?"

Judging by the way Atumbi's eyes bulged, the spirits
hadn't thought that aspect of the matter important
enough to mention; but the wizard made a quick re-
covery.

"Let them seek," he said. "If they should find the
shapes, there would be none left to trouble the lands of
the Wassabi."

"None of the shapes? Or of the Wassabi?"

Atumbi bristled. "None left of the whites, as Ktendi
knows."

"No, I do not know. I think Atumbi dissembles. His
people fear the shapes, as do we all. It is not good that
the whites should hunt them. More: this country be-
longs to us; it is virtually unknown to the whites; and
thus it should remain."

"That can be arranged," Atumbi said smugly.

"Thou art wrong, sorceror. If this safari finds even
one night shape, the Gundu lands will be overrun by
whites before two years have passed. Expeditions will
come by the handfuls to snare other such beasts, settlements will go up, there will be shootings and tram-
plings and spoilage, theft of women and corn and
property, torture and death in abundance. Atumbi, I
charge you, is this not only the truth?"

"It is a small truth," Atumbi said. "It is of no moment
to the Wassabi. Ktendi hath forbidden that the Wassabi
attack this safari, which is as white as he. Soon it will
be known that he fears only for his own small life; and
that his fine words mean only that his white brothers
might steal his stolen Wassabi gold. All this we scorn,
Ktendi. The Wassabi need not gold; they will protect
their own *bomas*, and will know Ktendi's cravings for
what they are. I have spoken. Enough."

"As have I," Kit said, rising. He stared down at the
plump shaman. "And I have said: *I will not have these
whites here*. Inevitably they will send runners to Atumbi

and consult with him, since they will think that Atumbi
knows better than we where the shapes might be found."

"That too is so," Atumbi said. "I see from your face,
Ktendi, an arrogance that little becomes a white. Think
you that the world contains only one valley where the
shapes live, and there only two or three? I know one
such valley that would affright you until you would
pray for a taking from Father Death. There, there are
tens and tens and tens of shapes. They all live there."

"And doubtless you also know where the elephants'
graveyard is," Kit said, with a short bark of laughter.
"Your threats are vile and horrid, fat man. Do you pro-
pose to tell these whites of this nest of shapes? Speak!
What do you threaten? What spites do you affright us
with?"

Atumbi spat disgustedly into the dust. Apparently
he had nothing further to say.

"Hear ye, sorcerer," Tombu said in a low voice, like
distant thunder. "If there exists another such valley,
and you know better than we or the whites where it is,
I tell you silence. Else I will send you into it naked of
even a spear. I your king say this; is it not so?"

"It is so," the magician said, in a voice of grinding
hatred. Tombu and Kit went out into the sunlight, leaving the shaman glumly regarding his piglet toes.

"Is there such a place?" Kit said, when they could
breathe again.

"Atumbi is full of lies; yet there might be. And if
there were, he might sell it. I do not see what we have
gained, Ktendi."

"Nothing yet. Only keep a close eye on the tribes.
Be sure that it is important to stop any attack upon
the safari now. Until we know more, silence and stealth
are our only hopes."

"Yes, *bwana,* but I cannot promise silence for Atumbi
without killing him," Tombu said quietly. "Or else he
will kill me, and return us to massacre and the cooking
of the long pig. This affair will give him fuel and tinder
among our people—and you leave me with nothing to
say that befits a king."

"I understand that," Kit said gently. "I'll remedy it

the moment I can. But I must leave it in your hands
now; I have other spears to harden, in the south."

The warrior king nodded. "Life, *bondele*."

"A thousand years."

Kit strode to the thorn gate. A thousand years—it
was a long time, the equivalent of an eternity for men;
but now, men were pushing into the deep Congo to
grapple with creatures which, they hoped, still lived
after the groaning passage of thirty thousand of those
terrible millenia. The Africans had better sense: they
had no word for "millions," for "thousands," or even for
"hundreds," for they knew that there were not so many
things in the world that were alike—not even years.

The whites, on the other hand, had the words and
the numbers. They also had the deaths that went with
them.

At the beginning of the second day's travel to the
south, Kit took to the trees; among other things, it kept
his feet dry. He had a long distance to go, and no changes
of boots to take with him; only his leathery, grasping
feet and hands. A canteen slapped at his left hip as he
climbed, containing a little water which was safe to
drink. Food was no problem, unless you were squeam-
ish—almost anything alive is good to eat, whether it
tastes good or not.

The drums hammered their gorilla chests incessantly, keeping the province informed of the move-
ments of the safari. Their sound was already becoming
angry and warlike:

Ktendi hath forbidden that the whites be molested.
The safari is a stirrer-up of demons.
The whites approach—
Ktendi hath forbidden—
They are daily closer to the valley—

Kit kept moving, south and west, roughly in the
direction of Lake Leopold. By nightfall the drums were
very dim, and no new, nearby hides picked up their
song-speech. Here what was urgent to the Gundu tribes
was matter of no moment. The land which was the land
of King Njona was no friend to Tombu and owed no
allegiance or friendship to Ktendi; it was even under

the thumb of Belgium only nominally, due to the good fortune—from Njona's point of view—which had vested most of the natural wealth of the Congo in the northern province of Katanga.

Kit waited until the jungle was blanketed in blackness, and then crept toward the *boma* within which Njona himself slept. Njona would be of no help, but that did not matter; he was not the one Kit was here to see. He waited again, until the cooking fires died, and the murmuring of voices dwindled and became blended with the whispering of the jungle.

Then he lifted his head and screamed.

It was a long, thin, rasping wail—a sound that should not have come from the throat of a man, or, better still, should never have been sounded at all. It was the mating scream of a panther.

And again, Kit waited. Through most of the village, Kit knew, Bantu women would be huddling their infants closer, and black warriors crouching tensely inside the woven mats which were the doors of their huts. That scream must have emptied the alleys and the big compound in a hurry—not so much as a precaution against the panther, a beast hated but not greatly feared in itself, as against any devil that might be choosing to use its voice as a mask.

And in one hut, a very old man would be waiting as Kit was waiting.

Kit found the hut without difficulty and scrambled at the reed mat, whining like a curious cat. A quavering voice said:

"Welcome."

It was pitch black inside, and there was no odor but the smell of earth, and a faint tang, half acrid, half musty, that suggested age. The quavering voice said:

"It is Ktendi, my sometime student. This matter of the valley is very serious, then."

"Deadly," Kit said. "Otherwise I would not trouble you, old one."

"I know that. Ktendi knows of the limits of my power. Within those limits, I may help; not beyond. What would he have me do?"

Kit squatted down and said tensely:

"First of all, there is a question of a second valley of which I have heard speech—a valley harboring night shapes in some numbers, not just one at a time. This is more reasonable on the face of it than that the creatures be solitary, and it will so seem to the white men when they too hear the tale."

"That is so."

"Then there is such a place, master?"

"Even so."

Paradoxically, Kit found himself breathing a little more easily. Up to now, he had been seriously in doubt of the wisdom of coming all this distance—and, in the process, turning his back upon an obviously explosive situation—on the strength of a threat from Atumbi, that fat liar.

"I am unable to order any attack on these whites," he said, "yet they cannot be allowed to reach this Valley. My desire that the safari be unmolested will quickly make me suspect among my own people; they may not do the important thing I must ask of them, when the time comes to ask it. I can see only one way."

"Speak."

"Njona hates you, but he fears more than he hates; it is widely known that you are a true sorcerer, and no leech. It must be said here in the village that Ktendi has deserted his people for the whites, and that the tribe of Tombu is weak and frightened."

The old voice said:

"Njona will make war on Tombu if this is said."

"Even so. That is what I wish. Within two days the people of Njona must go north, painted and armed, to war upon Tombu. The drums must cry war with great voices. Njona will ask omens of you; say him nay; he will be sure to go if you prophesy defeat." Kit paused, but the old shaman said nothing. Kit said, "This will be true prophesy, that you may make in all good faith."

"The word that Ktendi has betrayed Tombu will reach Tombu."

"No matter, Tombu will not believe it. Njona will, which will be all for the best. But there is more. There must be magic. This Ktendi cannot make."

"I make small magics. Speak."

Kit took a deep breath. "There must be a large magic. There must be lightnings in this Valley of Night Shapes. There must be lightnings—and fire."

For a long time it was silent in the stygian hut. For the first time since he had come to live in the jungle, Kit felt a nervous urge to make some useless motion—pull at his earlobe, shift his feet, anything to relieve the tension. If he had asked too much—

"That is great magic," the old man said. "Would Ktendi drive the beasts from their home? This must not be; the jungle would be very terrible if these grandfathers of serpents were abroad in it; more terrible if this were by our doing, since their home is their home and they have offered us no harm. Only to ask such a favor would not sweeten our names among the Powers. The whites would drive the shapes out; but we must not."

This was a virtual oration coming from the terse old sorcerer, and Kit knew that he had indeed overstepped the bounds of custom between master and student. Nevertheless, Kit drove forward.

"We must," he said, his voice deepening with conviction. "We must do more: we must drive the shapes directly over the camp of the whites, wherever that may be at the time. And then—we must drive them back into their Valley again."

The silence was eloquent.

"Look you, my master," Kit said. "We can bring no force to bear on the whites themselves, or we shall feel the whips on our backs before the year is out, the Gundu country will not be alone in ringing with gunfire, and the devil king in Belgium will be chopping off our hands like so many leaves. Our sole hope is to convince the safari that the great beasts have been driven out of their haunt and are scattered all over the face of Africa. There is no way to do that but to do it. And—of course the creatures must be driven back into the Valley again. Back, because, as you say, it is theirs; and driven, because they have not the cunning to find their own way."

"That is true. And so Ktendi means to muster the people of Njona and of Tombu at the rim of the fire, to herd the shapes to the Valley again, with the threat of war between the two tribes?"

"Yes," Kit said. "The flying things, if there are such, may return of their own accord when the fire is over; but the thunderers who walk must be herded. It will require us all to get them back, and there is no way but war to bring us together."

Once more there was a long silence. Then the old man said:

"You have the Sight, Ktendi, as once I foresaw you would. You say of the shapes words that are high secrets even among shamans; and well I know I never spoke them to you."

Kit permitted himself a brief sigh, and he hoped an inaudible one, of thanks for his past curious dips into Lyly's *Geology*.

"Then—can the lightnings be asked this favor?"

"The jungle is never dry; yet the season of rains is moons away. I will ask the favor, Ktendi—but it is a large magic for an old man. If I am refused, there will be slaughter between the tribes, and the whites will reach the Valley all the same."

"And Ktendi," Kit said wrily, "will go into the pot. My people have not forgotten the crisp crackle of long pig, for all that they have not tasted much of it since I came to them. It would be fitting if they broke my law with me."

"I will ask that there be a fire in the Valley, and say to you how to find it," the old voice said. "And ask also for a south wind to fan the fire. But this is a very large magic for such a man as I, Ktendi."

Kit stood up.

"I would not ask it," he said soberly, "of any other."

Two days gone by, and dusk again, and the trees purring and purling with an invisible river of wind. Kit paused in the crotch of a shea tree and listened. The safari had last been reported traveling the Ikatta, and he knew that it would have to leave that swampy river before it could get very deep into Gundu country.

A distant sound fought upward. Kit stiffened. *Singing?* For a moment he would not believe it. He wriggled

higher in the tree suffering a sudden eruption of ants
up one arm, and lay still along a thick, corded branch.

So the bearers still had spirit enough to sing? That
didn't jibe with the stories of whippings and desertions....

The deep bass voices drew nearer, and after a while
Kit could make out the language, and then—with great
difficulty—the words:

> "I die in the desert
> a thing accursed
> that saw thee,
> yet never possessed thee...."

No such song had ever been sung before in the Congo,
for there were no deserts anywhere in the immense
Belgian protectorate; only a very few patches of grassy
veldt in the northern highlands. Kit racked his mem-
ory. The dialect itself was utterly strange.

After a while he had the answer, supplied by the
words themselves; the attitude toward women they ex-
pressed would have seemed ridiculous to any Bantu;
but it was thoroughly Arabic—and the dialect fitted.
The expedition was using Turkana boys from Upper
Kenya, desert nomads who could never have heard any
of the legends of the jungle; whose language was so
heavily Semitic that they could talk to the Congo tribes
only with the greatest difficulty; whose traditions were
so fiercely individualistic that even in strange country
they would be managed only under the whip, and even
then would sing (though, to be sure, sad songs of exile
and loss; but did desert nomads have any other kind of
song?); and who could be depended upon not to desert.
Only the local recruits to the *poshi* would be likely to
drop out, and there could not have been very many of
them even at the start.

That was bad. There was obviously both money and
brains behind this raid on the jungle's oldest secret.

The rhythmic crashing of machetes had barely
reached Kit's ears when it was cut off. There was shouting, and then a vicious *crack!* which almost made him
wince. The headmen had whips, all right, and no re-

luctance about using them. Then a gleam of orange
showed that fires were being lit, and camp made for
the night.

Kit slithered forward, grasped the tough lianas, and
wormed his way ungracefully but silently into the next
tree. From here, he found that he could see a sizable
part of the encampment. Almost directly below him, a
tent was being pegged out, and before it three white
men stood, arguing in subdued voices. One of them held
the whip, doubled under his arm.

Off to one side, an incredibly thin, tall Negro was
patiently allowing his back to be taped by another white:
evidently the victim of the whip, getting a doctor's attention. The Negro confirmed Kit's guess. The man was
obviously a Turkan, a member of that small, conflictless
tribe which ranged the boundaries of the Kenya colony.

One of the white men raised his voice angrily.

"You're a fool," he said, in an Englishman's almost
intolerable French. "They'll take it from one of their
own kind, but from a white man it's another matter.
Haven't we lost enough bearers already?"

"I know what I'm doing," the man with the whip
growled. "France is full of niggers. If you allow them
an inch, they take an ell."

He swung suddenly toward the doctor and the tribesman and shouted an injunction so idiomatic, and so
transcendently obscene, that Kit was stunned that any
white man could have composed it; it was certainly not
anything he could ever have heard any Bantu say. The
man was a positive virtuoso in Swahili, of the kind
spoken by the Ubangi tribes; as for his French, it seemed
to be out of Bordeaux. He must have spent many years
in the south, in French Equatorial Africa, somewhere
in the vicinity of Bangui. That would account for the
form of address; and judging by the way he used the
whip, he might have spent the time there managing a
sisal-hemp plantation.

Regardless of the accuracy of these guesses, one thing
was plain: he was no amateur.

The doctor finished hastily and gave the tall Turkan
a slap on an unmarked shoulder. The boy went off with

a kind of surly patience, and the fourth white man joined the group before the tent.

"At least," he said, betraying himself at once as a Belgian, "try to take it a little easy, des Grieux. A welt is one thing, that doesn't cripple; but if you keep losing your temper and flaying the men, they're useless for weeks. Sometimes, for good."

"All right," the one called des Grieux said in a sour voice. "But I'm tired of all this malingering."

"So am I," the Englishman agreed fervently. "Listen to those damned drums! By the time we find the Valley at this rate, the whole country'll be up in arms."

"Those aren't war drums," des Grieux said contemptuously. "Just the usual information bureau. Dunstan, I thought you knew this country; but you spend half your time in a panic. What good is that, may I ask?"

"I know something about this part of the Congo," the man called Dunstan said in his atrocious French. "Which is more than you do. To begin with, I know that there's no such thing as a war drum, not up here: drums carry messages, and that's all. If they start carrying the war call, des Grieux, you'll have whipped it into being."

Kit decided that it was time he took a part in this conversation. Swinging his canvas boots over the edge of the branch, he slid away into the dark air and plummeted.

The men were still arguing when he struck, and the trampled grasses took up most of the sound of his landing. After a moment, the little doctor turned in Kit's direction as if to take himself out of the conversation in disgust. Then he started, and froze.

"What—Who's there?"

The others spun. Kit kept his thumbs inside his belt. Even in the fitful firelight, it should not be hard to see that he carried neither rifle nor spear—but more difficult to be sure whether or not there was a pistol under one of those thumbs.

He said:

"Good evening, gentlemen."

"My goodness," the doctor said, gasping like an asthmatic. "A white man—what a turn you gave me! How on earth—did you spring up out of the ground?"

"No, doctor, not exactly. I'm sorry I startled you. But I've had word of your safari, and I came to see you as fast as I could. I've some advice for you, if you're interested."

"Advice?" des Grieux growled. "We've got more than we need. Nobody here asked for yours, whoever you are."

Dunstan took him by the elbow. Des Grieux shook the grip off angrily, but the Englishman would not be forestalled.

"Just a minute, des Grieux," he said doggedly. "Control your bloody temper for ten seconds, will you? The man is trying to do you a favor."

"What of it?"

"Nothing of it," Dunstan said, throwing up his hands. "You are impossible. Don't you even know who he is?"

Des Grieux looked Kit over, carefully, and then shrugged. "No. But I'll listen."

"Unless I'm sadly mistaken," Dunstan said with the utmost caution, like a philosopher trying to construct a logical proposition which might stand for all time, "we have here the legendary Ktendi—Son of Wisdom, King of the Wassabi, Master of Serpents, and half a dozen other titles."

He was interrupted by an infuriate chorus of screams from a galaxy of monkeys, disturbed in their beds by, perhaps, a marauding snake. He waited patiently until the noise died. Then he said: "Sir, is that true?"

"I'm Kit Kennedy," Kit said.

"A stray hunter," des Grieux said. "Dunstan, in God's name keep your head. There's no such thing as Ktendi, and no such thing as night shapes, either. What we're hunting is dinosaurs, will you bear that in mind?—dinosaurs, real objects, real animals! Keep your damn romanticism to yourself! And as for you, Mr. Kennedy, why don't you mind your own business?"

"It is my business," Kit said. "Mr. Dunstan is right. I'm sorry to disappoint you, *M.* des Grieux, but there is a Ktendi. That's what the Wassabi call me. Would you like to argue the matter with them?"

The Frenchman simply shrugged, after the briefest of hesitations.

"What for?" he said. "I'm not interested in operatic heroes. I'm here on business, myself. If you're Ktendi, m'sieu, would you please state your business, and then get on back to your savages? We have neither the time nor the facilities to nurse parasites."

"Thank you," Kit said, with a smile of admiration. "But I don't need nursing. I'm here on your behalf, with nothing more to say than this: this is dangerous country you're entering."

"We know that."

"You know less about it than you think. I'd advise you to turn back."

"Oh?" des Grieux said coldly. "That's a threat, I presume?"

"Not at all. You are in no danger yet. But the tribes fear *juju* more than they do guns or whips. The Valley that you seek is held in great dread by all the Gundu tribes, and many others as well. If you persist in searching for it, you'll have a full-fledged revolt on your hands."

Des Grieux sniffed. "A real pretext to come in and civilize this morass, I'd say."

"It isn't your morass, des Grieux," the fourth white man broke in. It was the first time that he had spoken; and he sounded squeaking-angry. "This is the *Belgian* Congo, I remind you."

"True," des Grieux said. "Mr. Kennedy, you're a white man, I notice. You don't believe these stories about spirits and devils."

"You're wrong. I do."

"Please. I am not an idiot. I'm trying to be reasonable; will you give me a chance? What, for instance, is your interest in the Valley?"

"Personal."

"Naturally," des Grieux said. "But what is it?"

Kit said, "It's personal. That's all."

There was a long, itchy silence. At last, Dunstan said nervously: "Des Grieux, why can't you leave well enough alone? As the story goes, this man's an American who's taken to jungle living. That's his privilege. Maybe he just doesn't want us trespassing on his territory. Is that right, Mr. Kennedy?"

"Yes, Mr. Dunstan. In part, anyhow."

"His territory?" des Grieux laughed harshly. He strode forward, and shoved his face to within six inches of Kit's. "Listen, m'sieu. This is the King's territory— Leopold's, not yours. The last I heard, he had no regard for savages, no matter what their color."

"He's mistaken," Kit said quietly. "But I don't see what you're getting at, anyhow. You're not a Belgian."

"No. But I'm a hard-headed man—hard-headed enough to believe the unbelievable when the evidence is good. There are dinosaurs in this country. A man named Stahl told me he had seen one, and he's a reliable observer. I want drawings and specimens. I mean to get them. If the niggers fear magic more than guns, that is a very sad error on their part, and I'll re-educate them. Do you understand me?"

Kit calmly took des Grieux's nose between steel-hard fingers, and brought the astonished man to his knees with a merciless wrench of his wrist. Des Grieux tried to grab at Kit's legs, and missed. The whip fell to the ground. Kit put a foot on it, and bowled the man away from him.

"Your manners," he said, "need improving. I don't like people who puff in my face."

He scooped up the whip. Des Grieux scrambled back to his feet, raging; but if he had had any intention of charging Kit, the sight of the lash under Kit's arm seemed to change his mind.

Kit's eyes flicked over the guarded faces of the other white men. They did not seem disposed to interfere. In that brief silence, the pounding of the drum suddenly came rolling down over the encampment like a flood.

Dunstan stiffened. "That's it," he said, white-lipped. "That's a war call, or I've never heard one. Isn't that true, Mr. Kennedy?"

Kit cocked his head. The wild throbbing came from the north, where the lands of Tombu lay. It was a little garbled, but quite readable.

Ktendi hath betrayed the folk of Tombu.
Ktendi hath given the Gundu lands to Njona.
Ktendi hath promised the Valley to the whites.
Ktendi hath betrayed—
A word lost here. Then:

Spears to the south, or death! Spears to the south!

"Yes, Mr. Dunstan," Kit said. "That's what it is. Take warning, gentlemen. The natives war among themselves, and they'll keep it to themselves as long as you don't break their taboos. That specifically means the Valley of the Night Shapes. If you turn back now, you'll probably be safe—otherwise, you'll probably die."

"I am going to the Valley," des Grieux said, nursing his nose, and glaring malevolently over it at Kit. "That is what I came here for, and that is what I am going to do. The niggers don't scare me—and neither do you."

"All right," Kit said. "But *M*. des Grieux, the Valley is not a zoological garden. It's a place where old and deadly animals still live, animals that your world couldn't even tolerate—and things that we know better than you do. I assure you, if you fight your way through the tribes to the Valley, *you will wish you hadn't*."

As the last word left Kit's lips, there was a flutter of movement over his head. Then three tough, massive coils of cold power lashed about his waist, tightened, and lifted—

Manalendi!

The foilage closed about him. Below, the four faces looked up after him, white as milk.

The campfires dwindled behind them and blinked out. Kit clung rigidly to the python's flexing steel side for a moment, then hit it twice with his knuckles.

The coils froze, and then loosed him delicately. Kit crawled free and swung away into the tree. Below, there was a sudden hysterical shouting, and then a volley of shots through the tree they had just quit, whipping the leaves like heavy rain.

Kit kept moving. Only when he was sure that the campers could not hit him from where they were, even by accident, did he stop and catch his breath. The python's head glided to a stop nearby, but higher; though the animal weighed far more than Kit did, its weight was so evenly distributed that it could use far smaller branches.

"You're a melodramatic old sinner," Kit murmured. "What was the big idea, anyhow?"

The snake stirred uneasily; the sound of Kit's voice seemed to disturb it.

"What's the matter? Fighting somewhere?"

"*Tsssss,*" Manalendi said. He began to slide away. Kit waited curiously until the snake came back and drove a horny snout between his shoulder blades, nearly knocking him sprawling from the branch. Kit clutched at the vines and caught in a mouthful of air.

"All right, I'll come along. Don't be so damned persuasive."

"*Tssssssss!*" the snake said. It butted him urgently, and then began to travel again. Kit clambered after it as fast as he could. The drums boomed their war calls implacably; the very air seemed to shudder. After a while, Kit worked his way up to the top of a giant baobab to get a look at the stars. Manalendi traveled in a broad, impatient spiral of blackness around him, shaking the branches almost imperceptibly.

"We're going the wrong way," Kit muttered. "And it's clouding up. Look handsome, damned if I'll stop to steal you a shoat at this stage of the game. You'll get me lost, and I've got business at—*oof!*"

The snake's huge head had thudded into his ribs again. Kit decided to call a moratorium on his plans. Pythons normally sleep between meals—usually a week or more at a time. But Manalendi had something extraordinary on his cold little mind tonight, that was certain.

A distant flicker caught Kit's eye. For a moment he thought he had imagined it. Then it came again, unmistakably.

A chill went up Kit's backbone. It was several months too early for the rainy season, but that flash could mean only one thing: an old man in Njona's village had asked certain Powers a favor—and was going to get it, or at least some of it.

Well, that was how the Golden Rule went: *Ukimfaa mwenzio kwa jua, naye atakufaa kwa mvua*—Those who help in the wet season will have help in the dry. Still, it was eerie.

Kit clambered down and began to work south again. After a few moments, the snake followed. He was afraid that it would be disposed to interfere, but this time it made no protest.

This was doubly odd. Up to now, he had been being driven roughly in the direction of Balalondzy, toward that same valley which had once been Manalendi's home. It would have been impossible to reach it in anything under two weeks, but of course that was a notion impossible for Manalendi to entertain—as impossible as explaining to the python that everything of importance was now happening somewhere else. Now, however, the snake was letting Kit retrace his steps, which made no sense at all.

Or perhaps it was just as it should be. Basing one's plans on reading the mind of a python would not be very sensible, either.

He skirted des Grieux's camp, listening wryly to the sounds of frightened preparation that the drums had stirred up in it, and backtracked the safari. It seemed to be several hours later that he came upon the spoor of a large war party, but the stars were now completely overcast, and with them the passage of time; already Kit was beginning to wonder if the night would ever end.

The war party, when he reached it at last, was still on the move. They too were going south: therefore, probably Tombu's people, though Kit could not overhear enough talk to make sure. Not that it made much difference; Kit knew that neither side would be exactly glad to see him now. He passed on over them without making any sign, and when he was out of eashot, once more climbed to the top of a tall tree and looked north.

A dim haze of yellow and pink was glowing on the far, dark horizon. Whispers moved in the air above the tree tops—the flight of thousands of small, dark bodies. Most of them were birds. Kit had no desire to know what the others were.

He knew what he needed to know. The Valley was indeed on fire.

Kit descended to the middle reaches of the tree and waited. This was also as far as he intended to go, come what may. After a while, Manalendi butted him again— and then again, with pile-driver impatience.

"Cut that out," Kit growled. As the python's head wove toward him once more, Kit hammered it hard on the snout with the handle of his knife.

For once it was to trouble to reach Manalendi's mind. He was insulted. He swung away into the air, and came whistling back in a motion that would have been too fast to see even in bright daylight. Kit went sprawling off the branch like a rag doll. The universe spun once and disappeared.

Consciousness crept back, infinitely slowly, in a red haze of pain. Opening his eyes brought no change; it was still night. There was wet earth under him, and after a while he realized that he was wet all through. It was raining—not violently, indeed not hard enough to get through the treetop cover, but doggedly enough to fill the sable air with drippings from the leaves.

He moved tentatively, and had to bite his lips. Something was broken—a rib, at the least; perhaps two. Well, he had gotten off lightly. It had been a long fall—and Manalendi might just as well have killed him as knocked him down...

Speaking of that, where was the old sinner? Kit struggled to his feet, but it was impossible to see anything at all in the dripping blackness. Nor was he going to be able to do any more tree climbing, with his ribcage caved in like this; just breathing was painful.

The sky sheeted over briefly with lightning, showing as a stipple of blue-green mosaic pieces far aloft. The jungle was motionless in the brief, dubious light.

There was no sign of the python, which of course proved nothing. Kit wondered why it had suddenly decided that it wanted him to keep moving. Could it have been that he already sensed the fire? Naturally there was no way to find out—except, of course, to keep moving. He had expected Njona's party to pass him about here, but it was probable that the sudden storm had halted them; in which case he would have to go to them.

That could hardly have been Manalendi's reason for keeping in motion, but it was a good enough one for Kit. He started walking along the trail.

*   *   *

The encampment of Njona was not hard to find; with the ever-incredible Bantu failure to believe in the possibility of surprise attack, the warriors had lit fires.

Kit walked straight into it. Even a fallen king, he thought wryly, had a little presitge left—one can never tell when he might regain his throne. Besides, Manalendi might still be following him—a spectacle to give the most bloodthirsty enemy a sober second thought. Kit was not counting on that, however.

Njona came to meet him, tall and horrible in paint and feathers. His greeting was very simple. He said: "Go!"—two syllables in Swahili, and twice as unfriendly.

"I have grave news," Kit said, without giving any sign that he had heard the command. "Tombu's warriors are near."

Njona gestured imperiously with his spear. A Negro nearly as tall as himself stepped to his side.

"Make ready," Njona said. "The Wassabi approach." Then to Kit again: "Go. You are not wanted here."

Kit stood his ground; he knew his man. Njona no longer knew whether Kit was on his side or not; he was unfriendly, but not yet positively hostile.

"That is not the only word I bring," Kit said evenly. "It is now far too late to make war upon the Wassabi. Do you not hear the jungle?"

Njona lifted his head. The jungle was rustling with more than rain—only slightly, but perceptibly to a trained ear, once attention was called to it. While the black king listened, a small, vivid green snake shot through the splattered slime at his feet and vanished again, leaving behind a zigzag trail.

"The small ones first," Kit said softly. "Then the big constrictors, like my friend Manalendi of the Rocks. The birds have already gone over; perhaps you heard them, flying by night. And then—"

The chief's eyes bulged with realization. "The birds that fly by night" was a girot's drum-kenning for—

"Fire!" Njona said hoarsely. "Ktendi hath fired the jungle!"

"The fire began far from Ktendi," Kit said. "It began far beyond the villages of the Wassabi. It is—"

A medley of triumphant howls drowned him out. The underbrush shook, and erupted charging warriors. Njona's warriors snatched up their spears.

"The Wassabi!" Njona cried. He brushed past Kit. Arrows began to thrum from the trees around the clearing. On the north side, several men were already down, writhing. Shields thudded against each other.

At the same instant the trees were swarming with screaming monkeys, pushing at each other, biting, jumping wildly at branches they could not possibly make, dropping on the fighting men like the ripe baobab gourds that bore their name. The din was terrible; but above it a greater sound still came rolling in, a rising clamor of terror and death. The warriors hesitated, turning from each other, looking around and up—

A herd of wild beasts stampeded through the undergrowth, on hoofs as light as the footfalls of spirits. The glow on the sky was plainly visible now. The roaring and howling became still louder, and Kit thought he could hear the faint crackling of the flames themselves behind it; but it was hard to be sure.

The Africans forgot their war. "The trees!" Njona screamed. The ranks melted like clods in a flood, making for the thick trunks.

But it was already too late. There was terror up there among the leaves. A black and sinuous shape looked down at them from the nearest crotch, its eyes glowing green fury. Njona stabbed upward at it, and it responded with a sound like the death agonies of a devil. It was mad with fright and hatred, and sprang upon the instant, the sabers of its claws spread wide.

King and cat hit the ground simultaneously, but the panther did not stop to fight. It fled, a bolt of black lightning. In the tossing branches, more pairs of green slits flashed downward. The men slid back down the trunks again in a hurry.

"Tombu!" Kit shouted.

"Awa. Jambo, bwana."

The Wassabi chieftain, almost unrecognizable in his war clays, gestured from the other side of the clearing, but made no move to come closer. If he had, his own subjects would have put a spear in his back.

"The Valley has been burned out!" Kit proclaimed at the top of his voice. Even in the din he was sure that everyone could hear him. "The night shapes are coming this way!"

For an instant the shock froze them all. The sky was now bright enough to cast faint shadows. The ground shook with the passage of heavy bodies somewhere nearby—rhinos, possibly.

Then, slowly, Tombu approached. With him came two or three others, and Njona.

"Is this your doing, Ktendi?" Tombu said somberly.

"Yes, in part—but no matter. The great need now is to run ahead of the fire—it would be impossible to go against it anyhow—and herd the shapes directly over the camp of the whites."

"Herd *the shapes?*" Njona said, with the air of a man surprised for the first time in his life.

"Even so. It may not be needed, if the fire continues in that direction anyhow. That will show the whites what the shapes are like, enough to satisfy them all their lives long—if they live through it all. They will go home and report that the great things have been scattered beyond hope of capture. *But they must not stay scattered.*"

Both chieftains nodded in unison. That went without question. Penned in the Valley, the night shapes lived out their immortal lives without much infringing upon the lands of men and beasts; but roaming abroad—no, that could not be suffered.

"I have three hundred men," Njona said.

Tombu grinned mirthlessly. "So many? It is well this war was stopped. I have half that many, Ktendi. It is enough?"

"It will have to be. We had better fan out. The forest folk won't molest us unless we try to halt them; let them by."

He moistened a finger. The fire seemed to be moving a little to the east of them, under the urging of a steady, inexplicably cold wind. When Njona's shaman, who made small magics, asked certain Powers a favor, he evidently was given it in brimming measure. Kit knew instinctively that was probably the first such favor the

old man had ever asked—and certainly the last he would
be granted.

"This is good. The shapes will go to the west. It would
be impossible to make them go back into the blaze."

There was a new thunder, agitating the huge trees
like the pebbles in a witch doctor's rattle. The night
rang with the trumpeting of elephants.

The noise got louder. It was impossible, but it was
so.

On the yellow-lit loam, the night shapes came lumbering. Branches snapped like sparks at their approach.

They were hard to see—and it was impossible to
believe what one saw. The first to come through was a
thirty-foot gray-green tower with a wide-fanged head,
blundering like a kangaroo upon vast hind legs. It froze
Kit to the ground, his muscles congealed with panic.
Somehow he had never dreamed that these monsters
might be five times as tall as he was.

Then the thing moved forward, and Kit forced himself to shout at it. It stopped, and glittering, mindless
eyes looked down at the puny figure with the brand.
The eyes, as big and muddy as oysters, blinked with
mechanical regularity.

Brand. Fire.

The shape was stupid, however terrible. It could not
differentiate between a torch and a conflagration. After
a while its walnut-sized brain turned it away and sent
it striding vastly, clumsily toward the west.

There were more. The world became an endless
nightmare.

There were four-legged monsters twice the size of
hippos, with ridges of flat spear-blades along their backs,
like the river beast Manalendi had fought. There were
screaming, eighty-foot nightmares with necks and tails
as long each as Manalendi, legs like tree trunks, bodies
that would have dwarfed a bull elephant. There were
wide scarlet maws, lashing tails that bore batteries of
spikes, great turtlelike carapaces, grasping four-fin-
gered paws with thumbs as cruel as thorns, pads that
mashed five inches into the mud at every step. Above,
in the lurid light and the smoky columns of rain,
wheeled shapes like bats—shapes with wings as big as

sails—wheeling and calling to each other hoarsely, eagerly.

And there were shapes for which no words existed, shapes older than words, shapes older than the walking apes who had invented words. Among them, anonymous forever, *mokele-mbemba*.

The men were Johnny-come-latelies. They had nothing but spears, arrows, fire and courage.

Also, they had brains.

The nonstop, obscene nightmare lasted a week, and might well have lasted forever had not the eternally wet jungle been so intolerant of the fire. That was brought to an end by an early torrent of the rainy season—perhaps one last favor from the Powers.

Kit wasted no time speculating about that. He had had no sleep, except for minutes here and there. He was not thinking at all anymore—only reacting. Exactly as some girl or other had once told him he did usually.

Nothing could be done, it had turned out, to turn the shapes back toward their home Valley. They were too far from that home. But they had begun to bunch again near Balalondzy, and there seemed to catch a scent that they knew. From then on it was no longer a matter of herding them, but only of keeping up with them; they were going like so many scores of juggernauts toward that other valley where Kit had once danced on a drum.

This had been no part of Kit's plans, but he decided it suited him. There was only one way for the shapes to get into *that* valley, and that was by way of the river's mouth. By the same token, that was the only way they could get out of it, too—and that could be prevented.

He felt no particular concern for the village where he had danced. He rather doubted that it was even in existence anymore, after the battering it had taken and the rout of its slave masters. He did wonder, vaguely, whether or not there would be enough to eat in the valley for so many voracious reptiles; though their numbers had been much reduced, both by fire and by bullets—that almost unmanagable Special of des Grieux's had turned out to be able to fell them very well indeed, and the Belgian had stood his ground with it to the last—it struck him that just one such appetite per valley would be the soundest arrangement. Well, it couldn't be helped.

The party paused at the edge of the veldt. Though it was nearly nightfall, this was familiar territory; they had camped here before. It was time, at last, for a break. Tombu had already staked it out and gotten things organized.

"You do not want to keep following?" the chieftain said, motioning with his head out across the trampled grassland.

"No. We know where they've gone. If they decide to come out again, we'll hear it quickly enough. But I doubt that they will."

"Even so."

Kit sighed. Nearby, he heard the boys talking among themselves. They must be as tired as he, but the wonder and fear of what they had seen—and what they had managed to do—was still moving them.

"*Munti nini abumi njoku oyo?*"

"*Mondele na yo te?*"

"*Seju.*"

And then, a fragment of another conversation:

"*Wapi ye?*"

"*Ktendi alobi ye akuya te.*"

"*Je nina akuya te?*"

"*Manalendi. Bango bandeko na Ktendi.*"

That would have been interesting, had Kit not been so tired. It was not very surprising that the Wassabi thought of the python as being, at least in a sense, one of the night shapes; but the last speaker had used the plural form—"*They* are the friends of Ktendi." How on earth could they have reached that conclusion?

It didn't matter. He turned toward his sleeping tree—the very same tree, in fact, in which he had first met Manalendi. Tombu was standing there, watching him and grinning. Kit felt vaguely alarmed; the things that amused the African had a tendency to be violent.

"What's the joke, Tombu?"

"Nothing, Ktendi. *Ay-obwa. Baminga; nansima ma-camba yonso cakosilisa.*"

"*Baminga,*" Kit said, and began to climb. The African's benediction—"Afterwards all the troubles will be over"—was only a piety, but it was a nice thought to go to sleep on.

The boys had, he discovered, built him a rude platform up here, and for once he felt that he needed it. There was even a lump of bedding, quite a sizable one by his standards. He seated himself on the edge of the boards, and in the fast-falling night, began to loosen his boots.

Behind him, a voice said quietly:

"Oyo esika biso tolalaki."

He turned, very slowly. It was not the words that stunned him, they were only simple observation. It was the voice.

Paula sat up. She said nothing further. Her face was very pale.

"Yes," Kit said, in French. He knew her Swahili was not good; in fact, she had once declared that she hated the language. "Yes, we have slept here before. But—how did you get here? What are you doing?"

"It was Tombu's idea of a joke. He kept me carefully hidden all this time, and spirited me up here about an hour ago. I'll go if you like, Kit."

"Where would you go?"

"Back where I came from."

Kit snorted. She made it sound like catching a trolley. His whole spirit was entirely too numb to cope with this problem. His opinion of Tombu's jokes fell still another notch.

"What do you mean by 'all this time'?" he demanded. "Since when? What are you up to?"

"Never mind." She threw the bedding off and swung her feet over the edge of the platform. It wasn't a far drop; she could jump it easily. "I didn't think it was a good idea, myself. *Baminga,* Ktendi."

"No, wait." He clutched desperately at his head. If only he could think! "Please, Paula. I'm sorry to be rude. I'm almost always rude, as you well know. I'll stop grilling you. I just want to know how this happened."

"Fair enough," she said; but she still had her back to him, and it was very straight. "I was in des Grieux's party. When all those—when the safari broke up, Tombu made a quick side trip around our camp to loot guns and medicines, and came across me. He thought springing me on you at the very last minute would be a great climax to the whole affair for his *bondele*. He gave me a special *poshi* that kept me trailing along behind until last night—then they rushed me up ahead of you, and here I am."

"I see," Kit said, but it was only an automatic noise. The whole thing was as total a mystery as before. "Well...I'm glad to see you."

"Thank you."

"Dammit, I mean it. But I'm still mystified. I never dreamed you'd come within an ocean of Africa again, let alone here."

"I couldn't help it," Paula said quietly. "You made a savage of me, Kit. I'm a pretty sorry sort of savage, and I know it, but that's what I am. I was no good for tea-and-crumpets at Whitehall any longer. And of course everyone knew the story, and they knew I was a savage, too. They knew it before I did."

Kit felt a dull ache, half sorrow, half guilt, spreading through him. "I'm sorry," he said. "The worst of it is, all along I had the feeling that it would be something like that."

She turned suddenly. "No, no! It's not your fault! You told me! That was what we were always quarreling about. It's that I wouldn't listen! I had to learn some other way. And after a while, I—I decided I had to come back. When des Grieux asked me to join the party, because he thought I knew where the Valley was, I said yes."

"Hmm. He was thinking of *this* valley, of course."

"Yes. But I could never have found even this one. It was just a pretext. I thought I could get away from him as soon as we got into your part of the country—but he knew I was up to something. I never had a chance...not until all those horrors came thundering over us, and Tombu found me."

She shuddered convulsively. Kit reached across the tiny square of boards and pulled her to him.

"It's all right. You're safe now. I just may clout Tombu

one for this trick, but nothing will happen to you. I promise."

She sighed raggedly, and was silent for what seemed to be a long while. Then she said:

"I'm not afraid. Isn't that odd? But it's true, I'm not afraid. I made up my mind before I left that I didn't care how it came out, I was coming back to—here. It could take me in, or it could kill me. I knew that. I would have welcomed either."

"Hush." He kissed her. Below, the boys began to hum...a long, winding song in imitation of a drum message, which had no words because one could hear the words in the tune.

"Paula."

She stirred, and rested her forehead against his neck. "Yes."

"This isn't over yet. Will you stay in camp tomorrow, until I come back?"

"If you'll come back."

"Yes."

"Nansima macamba yonso cakosilisa."

"Where have you been picking up the language? You used to hate it."

"No, my dear," she said. "I didn't hate it. I hated you. Actually it's a beautiful language—I could hear that right away."

"Well," Kit said, ruefully, "one thing is still in character. Your accent is dreadful."

Paula tipped her head back and laughed at the stars. "Thank you," she said. "Now I know I'm home—the man's insulting me again."

Something stirred under the massive frown of the cliff. A huge, heavy head wove up over the treetops, which were low here because the ground was too soaked to allow enough roothold for a really big tree.

Nevertheless that head was far above them in the dawn sky. It bobbed from side to side restlessly, and then turned to look down at them.

Bowstrings twanged, and a black flight of arrows whined around the great snout. Kit held the Davidson aimed steadily at the beast's throat.

But it was not needed. The shape hissed, like a teakettle, an almost comically small sound, and went lumbering back upriver.

"That's the last," Kit said. His throat was still roughened with smoke and fatigue. "I hadn't counted on a latecomer."

"It is wounded," Tombu said.

"Yes. I'm sorry so many got killed. Well, the hyenas and the vultures will clean them up—in a while. And then we must bury the bones, or this whole tale will be told all over again. Who has a brand?"

There were several in the party. One was passed from hand to hand until it reached Kit. He took it and went forward into the pass, looking up at the great overhang, feeling a slow, solemn, almost inhuman regret for what had to be done.

The three white sticks slipped neatly into the crevice he had chosen. Kit wound the fuses together, lit the longest one and ran. At the count of eight he threw himself on his face.

The blast sent fragments of rock and green wood whoo-whooing wildly through the morning mist. The overhang tottered. Then, majestically, it came down, and an avalanche of rubble came after it. The sky was abruptly extinguished by a burgeoning cloud of rock dust.

The roar of that avalanche died at long last, leaving nothing behind in Kit's ears but the ringing howl of deafness. He got up, slowly, looking at the shambles. There was no longer even a river at his feet.

He was too stunned to realize what this meant, for long minutes. Then, as his hearing returned, he began to hear the sound of the water, circling and circling . . .

How long would the dam last? There was no way to tell. The river was big, and powerful—but it was swirling now against uncountable tons of stone. If it lasted only a year, the shapes would drown, all of them. If it did not stand that long, the shapes would be killed in the torrent when it broke. Knowing the power of water over stone, Kit was prepared to bet upon the torrent.

Either way, the world would never see the shapes again.

"Tombu," he said heavily, "let's go home."

* * *

Yet it had to be done; and it had been done. Kit clambered back into the tree with its small square of boards as to a haven; and indeed he felt oddly, almost disturbingly at peace with himself, as though he had suddenly grown old.

Paula was waiting; and after a while, Kit discovered that the peace was real.

"It's over," he said. "It's really over. There may be something else tomorrow, but this one is done."

Paula drew her breath in, tranquilly, to reply. At that very last of all the instants Kit had been waiting for, his whole body turned into a steel statue of itself.

"Kit! What's—"

"Listen."

It came closer, and passed at its leisure over their heads: a slow, leathery flapping of great wings.

"Kit—is that—"

"Yes. It's one of them."

The flapping diminished, going toward the valley.

"Kit, they're all coming here. Even the—ones that fly. Even those may never come out again. There are so few of them left...how can they last? We've killed them off—maybe not just now. But they can't last. They're too old, and too few."

"Yes," Kit said heavily. "I think that's right."

But she heard the tone rather than the words, and huddled against him. "Then—what's wrong?"

He cradled her, wondering how to say it, or whether to say it at all. But she was with him now. She would have to know.

"The beasts in the valley may die," he said in a remote voice. "I think they will. The night shapes are another story entirely. They can never die. The night shapes aren't animals, or men, or demons, even to begin with. They're the ideas of evil for which those real things only stand. The real things are temporary. They can be hunted. But the shapes are inside us. They've always lived there. They always will."

The girl clung to him, unable to stop listening, unwilling to believe. After only a little while, he discovered that she was asleep, as sweetly as a child. He composed her gently, and lifted a heavy head to look at the star-bitten night.

Manalendi looked back at him.

Appendix

Terms and Phrases

(Everyone's literary usage of Swahili is idiosyncratic, there being as yet no standard spelling and no "classical" form of the language, which is of course subject to innumerable regional variations. My usage generally follows that of the dedicatees who compiled the first English-Swahili dictionary in the field shortly after the time in which the action of the novel takes place.)

Aka na yango. Go to it.
askari. Gun-bearers.
awa. Here.
ayang. Attack.
Ay-obwa. Nothing is wrong.

bafumba. Driver ants.
baminga. Peace.
Bango bandeko na X. They are the friends of X.

bendele (or *bondele)*. White man.
Bendele bafa banto. White men are not people.
boma. A wall.
bondoki. Rifles.

capita. Head boy.

Endoka tofa la bonyolo. Here we have no chains to
   bind you.

girot. Message-drummer.

Ibwa wete joi ja nkakamwa. Death is a strange thing.

jambo. Hail, hello, health.
Je adjali. He is there.
Je makasi. He is strong.
Je nina akuya te? Who is it that will never come?
jilo. Meat-hunger.
juju. Magic (or, religion).

kraal. Camp or village.
Kosala pila moko ngai koloba. Do it as I say.
kwashiorkor. Malignant malnutrition.

linginda. A fishing net.
Lokuta te. That is no lie.

Makili mingi. There is much blood.
malamu. Go.
matabische. Tip, reward, honorarium, present.
mbote. Live (a greeting).
Mnai djuna. Don't touch me.
mondele. Sir, boss, white man.
Mondele alobi ye akuya te. The boss says he will never
   come.
Mondele na yo te. Didn't the boss do it?
mpifo. Face, pride, station.
Mpo-kuseya. I cannot (fail).
Munti nini abumi njoku oyo? Who killed all those
   animals?

Nansima macamba yonso cakosilisa. Afterward all the troubles will be over.

ngoma. Ritual, ceremony, orgy.

nibo. King.

nyama. Meat.

Oyo esiki biso tolalaki. This is the place where we slept.

poshi. Guard.

Seju. I don't know.

sjambok. A short whip or cane.

tika. Wait.

Ukimfaa mwenzio kwa jua, naye atakufaa kwa mvua. If you help somebody during the dry season, he may help you during the rainy season.

Wapi ye. Where is he?

Winner of the HUGO AWARD
JAMES BLISH

NIGHT SHAPES   64675-7/$2.50

This is the story of American ex-patriot Kit Kennedy who inhabits the darkest part of the planet, where the past and future clash in a midnight of phatasmagoria of illusion and reality.

WELCOME TO MARS   63347-7/$2.50

When 18-year-old Dolph Haertel discovers the secret of anti-gravity, he journeys to Mars in his home-made space ship, and becomes marooned there when his power tubes are destroyed during his landing. He must quickly discover the secret to survival on the strange planet—or perish.

FALLEN STAR   62463-X/$2.50

An expedition team at the North pole searches for evidence of a war between Mars and a now-annihilated planet. Their quest leads to death, the discovery of an alien in their midst, and to the frightening realization that their own planet's continued existence is now in jeopardy.

JACK OF EAGLES   61150-3/$2.75

A fast-paced science fiction-ESP novel, first published in the 1950's and now considered a classic, in which an average New York copywriter suddenly realizes that he has ESP, and is plunged into a dangerous world of madmen bent on world domination.

DOCTOR MIRABILIS   60335-7/$2.95

In this classic novel, Blish vividly captures the life of Roger Bacon, the brilliant and eccentric philosopher whose radical teachings and heretical scientific theories led to his persecution at the hands of the 13th century Catholic Church.

BLACK EASTER   59568-0/$2.50

Theron Ware, the black magician and most satanic wizard on Earth, is told to unleash the demons of Hell, just for one evening. But when all Hell breaks loose, Earth becomes the site of the most unimaginable horror...

THE DAY AFTER JUDGMENT   59527-3/$2.50
The powerful sequel to BLACK EASTER, in which the survivors of World War III awake to find Satan ruling the Earth, and become caught in the ultimate battle between good and evil.

CITIES IN FLIGHT   58602-9/$3.50
AT LAST THE FOUR NOVELS IN ONE VOLUME!
A perennial best-seller, CITIES IN FLIGHT is a science fiction classic. In this tetralogy, the author has structured an entire universe in which mankind is no longer bound to the solar system, but has become both conqueror and victim of the stars.

THE STAR DWELLERS   57976-6/$1.95
When a life form as old as the universe is discovered, its tremendous energy could be of great use on Earth, and man is faced, for the first time, with the implications of trusting an alien creature.

MISSION TO THE HEART STARS   57968-5/$1.95
In this sequel to THE STAR DWELLERS, the Angels, a tremendous energy form, have signed a treaty with humans. But their peaceful co-existence is threatened when a civilization at the center of the galaxy tries to make earth a "subject state."

TITANS' DAUGHTER   56929-9/$1.95
Sena, the blond blue-eyed heroine, is a tetrapoid giantess—taller, stronger, longer-lived, than "normal" men and women. For Sena, who was not yet thirty, the whole world was in the throes of an endless springtime of youth that would last more than a century. But would the jealous "normals" let her live?

AND ALL THE STARS A STAGE   61739-0/$2.25
When the sun explodes, all life will end. No one will survive the blow-up; except the men and women who crowd into a few starships and fly away into space while there is still time, to look for a new home in the infinite void, a new planet on which to settle.

If you like Heinlein, will you love Van Vogt?

A READER'S GUIDE TO SCIENCE FICTION

by Baird Searles, Martin Last, Beth Meacham, and Michael Franklin

Here is a comprehensive and fascinating source book for every reader of science fiction — from the novice to the discerning devotee. Its invaluable guidance includes:

*A comprehensive listing of over 200 past and present authors, with a profile of the author's style, his works, and other suggested writers the reader might enjoy

*An index to Hugo and Nebula Award winners, in the categories of novel, novelette, and short story

*An outstanding basic reading list highlighting the history and various kinds of science fiction

*A concise and entertaining look at the roots of Science Fiction and the literature into which it has evolved today.

"A clear, well-organized introduction."
                              Washington Post Book World

"A valuable reference work."   Starship

Available wherever paperbacks are sold or directly from the publisher. Include $1.00 per copy for postage and handling; allow 6-8 weeks for delivery. Avon Books, Dept BP, Box 767, Rte 2, Dresden, TN 38225.

AVON Paperback   **46128-5 / $2.95**

GSciFi 12-82